Praise for *The Eunuch's Daughter*

Short, jewel-like chapters, evocative and layered. A beautifully written book.

Roundfire Books

The Eunuch's Daughter is indeed a beautiful book: extraordinary writing, interesting characters and a fascinating depiction of Vietnam's history.

Washington Writers' Publishing House

It is a remarkable story – ambitious, sweeping, and very beautiful. A gorgeous story as complex as Russian nesting dolls. An incredibly beautiful and compelling read.

Alexis Gargagliano
(former *Scribner*'s Editor)

Khanh Ha's latest work, *The Eunuch's Daughter & Stories* may be his best effort to date. He's a writer of rare talent able to plumb the depth of the human heart in the smooth rhythm of a meandering river. Ha steers the reader through the currents of history, heartbreak, and human dignity like a master riverboat captain. The writing is so smooth, so fluid, that the audience, entranced by the passing landscape, will not realize there is someone steering the boat. The visual is so vivid that the mystery and beauty of existence ripple up from the deepest of depths.

Ha's work always put me in mind of Faulkner in that it has a mythic quality that only the best writers are able to capture. At the same time, it is – at times brutally – realistic. As in all of Ha's work, there is something redemptive at play, something hopeful in tragedy, something dignified in sorrow.

In short, these stories are beautiful. I can't recommend *The Eunuch's Daughter & Stories* highly enough.

John Gist, author of
The Yewberry Way: Book I Prayer,
Lizard Dreaming of Birds, and *Crowheart*

CONTENTS

The Eunuch's Daughter   1
A Yellow Rose for the Sinner   111
The Yin World of Love   131
The Weaver of Điện Biên Phủ   143
Destination Unknown   159
Two Shores   177

The Eunuch's Daughter
& Stories

KHANH HA

Acknowledgments

Portions of this collection have previously appeared in somewhat different form in the following publications: *Superstition Review, Red Wheelbarrow Review, Outside in Literary & Travel Magazine, Solstice Magazine, Evening Street Review, Cutleaf Journal, Saint Ann's Review,* and *Blackwater Press Short Story Collection* 2022. The feature story has been adapted from the novel *Her: The Flame Tree* (Gival Press, 2023).

The Eunuch's Daughter

One

A black-and-white photograph fell out of the sheets of the novel. April picked up the photograph and asked, "Who is she, Minh?"

I looked up from my desk. "Someone in the past, from Vietnam."

My wife turned the photograph over. There was nothing written on the back, I knew. "Your ex-girlfriend?"

"No, no, she's twice my age."

My wife, unconvinced, frowned. "She looks young, and un-Vietnamese."

"She's half French, half Vietnamese."

"What's her name?"

"Phượng."

"*Foong?*"

"Yes. *Foong,*" I said, echoing her accent. "It means the flame tree in Vietnamese."

"Tell me about her."

So I told my beloved wife, a Virginia native, that one day, long ago, when I was a young writer looking for material in the Purple Forbidden City of Huế, I came upon an old Vietnamese magazine article about a centenarian eunuch of the Imperial Court of Huế. He had died in 1968, two years before I was born. The writer had interviewed the eunuch's adopted daughter. At the end of the article was a small halftone photograph of

3

her. The story had lodged deep in my brain. Months later I realized that it wasn't the story that was haunting me – it was the face in the photograph.

* * *

Phượng.

Dawn or dusk, you could see mottled-brown sand-pipers running along the seashore, legs twinkling, look-ing for food. Twilight falling. I followed their tracks, like twiggy skeletons strewn across the marbled sand until they ended under the frothing waves. One delicate bird stood at the water's edge and gave out a cry.

I often think of Miss Phượng as that sandpiper stand-ing at the edge of the sea, its cry lost in the sound of the waves.

two

The sugarcane field was so still in the summer afternoon heat you could hear the rustle of leaves beneath the lull of cicadas.

"Take my hand," Miss Phượng said to me. "Let's get off the blacktop road. Take this dirt trail. It wasn't here – twenty some years ago, that night. Now, you see over there, those huts in the middle of the field where they make syrup and block sugar. There was nothing there back then but sugarcane, this whole field."

Miss Phượng wore sepia cotton pants, the color of the dirt trail. Her short-sleeved shirt was so white its

glare made you squint.

"Please tell me your name again. Minh? I hope you will forgive my failing memory. On a good day, I am myself. Let's stop here. Where you can still see the road. Here I found him. Jonathan Edward. He was young. Like you, Minh. I don't remember the year. Perhaps 1965. I was twenty-three. He came here, half the world away, like you. Could be this spot. I'm not sure. But it was here where I held him, sitting right here, cradling his head in my arms, as he died."

three

Miss Phượng met the last concubine of Emperor Tự Đức when the woman was very old, in the final year of her long life. When the emperor died, in 1883, she was only fifteen. She told Miss Phượng she was one hundred and twenty-three. Small, birdlike, white hair parted in the middle, braided in two small plaits on the sides of her head.

She took Miss Phượng by the hand and led her into the cottage, which stood behind a bamboo hedge in the back of the mausoleum. She served tea from a tiny blue-flowered pot the size of her hand. The nougats she offered were made of egg whites and brown sugar and chopped nuts. Brittle, they melted quickly in the mouth.

"I used to make them for the emperor," she told Miss Phượng. "A long time ago." Then regarding Miss Phượng, she nodded, "Do you see the banyan out there?"

It dwarfed the cottage with its shade, like an immense pavilion. Miss Phượng traced its tortuous roots to the steps of the concubine's home.

"It was but a little tree when I came," the old woman muttered.

"Yes," Miss Phượng said, "trees outlive us. My father had a magnolia planted outside the Trinh Minh Palace during his service as the grand eunuch for the imperial family. He would be three years older than you, Madam, if he still lived."

In the deceased emperor's personal room, the old concubine sat down on the carved rosewood bed. Hunched between the parted panels of the yellow mosquito net, she sat amidst her husband's belongings: the bed, its embroidered mat, the porcelain pillow, the tea, the rice liquor, the areca nuts and betel leaves, and a tiny pot of lime. They were there for him when he returned in spirit.

For one hundred and eight years she replenished them every morning so that when he arrived nothing was missing, nothing was stale. He could read his favorite books. He could write, as was his passion, in his annals, each page of which was a thin leaf of gold. He would find again his gold swords, jade shrubs, his chess men in green and white jade, chopsticks made of *kim-giao* white wood that turned black against any sort of poison. They were arranged there under glass.

Miss Phượng took the old woman's hand and led her out of her haunt, passing candlelit nooks and corners, and the eternally mildewed air of the sunless chambers.

* * *

Miss Phượng thought she heard a baby cry in her sleep.

Waking, she opened the window. A breeze blew in across the dark back court beyond which lay the flagstone walkway under the shade of Indian almond trees. When was the last time she had heard a baby cry? This house had no nursery, no mother who lulled her child to sleep with her lullaby. But she could still hear it. She knew of superstitions. The indelible belief in animism. An unseen presence dwelling in an odd-looking rock by the roadside where people placed a bowl of rice grains and a stick of incense long gone cold.

She lit the oil lamp and sat down on a cane-backed chair. The smoky odor. The trembling shadows. What day is today? It must be an even day, for there is no electricity. But the helping girl, before leaving for the day, had made sure the oil lamp was full of kerosene. The matchbox too was packed with ivory-yellow sticks. Out of a terracotta crock she picked a preserved persimmon, round, palm-sized, dusted white with flour to keep it dry. Its amber skin was like aged cognac. Hunger made her weak in the limbs. She ate, chewing slowly. She remembered the dark, sweet flavor. What is the name of this fruit? she asked herself.

In the lidded jar of China blue lay slivers of cinnamon bark. Rice papers, cut into small round pieces the size of a centime, which sometimes had black sesame seeds in them and a fragrance. Her father, wearing his funny-looking eunuch hat with a mouse's tail on the back, had said to her, "Phượng, this is your favorite," as he turned the rice-paper snacks over the fire. Blistered and browned, she ate them and their wholesome aroma would linger on her fingertips.

four

"*Chú oi!*"

Over me a haloed figure stood silhouetted against the sun's glare. A girl's face slowly came into focus. I pushed myself up, my back warmed by the stone well behind the inn in the rising morning heat. The helping girl looked down at me.

"Why are you sleeping out here?"

"A centipede crawled on my face last night."

The girl slowly sat down on her haunches. The briny air fanned my face.

"So, I turned on the light," I said. "No electricity. Used my Zippo and guess what I saw on the floor? Cock-roaches. Bigger than my big toe."

"So? Every house has them, chú."

She called me uncle. I was only twenty-three. I couldn't tell her age though, for she had a thin body of a child and a woman's face. Her long-lashed eyes brooded. A small mouth that seldom smiled. When she did, a dim-pled smile brightened her face. Sometimes she laughed. Flutey laughs. She wore a red kerchief around her head. "Daddy makes me wear it so sand won't get in my hair," she once said to me. "So I don't have to wash it every day." She wore her hair past her shoulders, sometimes in two plaits, as I would have the chance to notice.

"I forgot to ask. What's your name?" I asked.

She said nothing.

"Everyone has a name," I said, bringing my knees to my chest and plugging a cigarette between my lips. She watched me click open my Zippo, her gaze following my hand. I blew the smoke upward. "You remember my

9

name?"

"Yes, chú."

"Say it."

"Minh."

I blew a series of small rings toward her. I saw her smile.

"That's pretty," she said, lifting her face to see where the rings went.

"You forgot your name? You not yourself today?"

"That's not funny."

I tapped the ash and saw it drift and cling to her peach-yellow blouse in gray specks.

"I'm sorry," I said. "Let me."

She shrank back. "Daddy smokes too," she said, flicking her gaze at me. "But he never takes the cigarettes out of his mouth. He has ashe all over his shirts. It burns holes in them."

I flicked open the Zippo then clicked it shut. "What does he do for a living?"

"He's a fisherman."

She held herself still, hands clutching the hem of her blouse to hold the scattered ashes. She looked up at me and grinned mischievously.

I shook my head. "What do I call you?"

"Does it matter?" she said.

"I don't even know how old you are."

"Do you have to know?"

"Sure, if you want to be my friend."

"I have friends. And we don't care how old we are. We never ask."

I rolled my eyes and took a last drag. I looked at the long, salmon burn on her left cheek. "How'd you get burned there?" I asked, pointing to my cheek.

She shook her head.

"It's a different culture here, eh," I said.

"What are you saying? Aren't you Vietnamese too, chú?"

"Yeah, I am. But I left Vietnam when I was seven."

"You told me you're a Vietnamese American."

"I grew up over there."

"How come you speak Vietnamese so well?"

"Because my parents are Vietnamese," I said, grinning, and it seemed to irk her.

"Are you really from America?"

Now I stared at her as I lit another cigarette.

"Prove it," she said.

I was about to tell her to forget it, but then, with a sigh, I dug my driver's license out of my wallet. "Here."

She leaned forward, her eyebrows knitted in appraisal.

"Can you read English?" I asked.

Her lips stopped moving. She flipped the plastic sleeve, stopped at the next one. Her head canted to one side. "Who is she?"

"My girlfriend."

"She's pretty. Her hair's not yellow though."

"She's a brunette."

"What's her name?" She perked up.

"Do you have to know?"

She pushed away my hand. "You're mean," she said sharply. "I hate you."

On the table that sat under the eaves of the rear veranda was a brass pail. It was half-full with well water. A tin can floated in it. I dipped the water with the can, rinsed my mouth, gargling, and brushed my teeth. With the water left in the pail, I washed my hair.

"You don't have long hair like me," she said. "Why

waste water?"

"I've got sand in my hair," I said, combing the wet strands back with my fingers. "I was down on the beach last night. So windy. You should wash your hair every day too."

"Easy for you to say, chú. Clean water here is treasured like rice to every family."

"Where do you get your water?"

"From a public well." She glanced toward the lodging house's well. "It has a pump like that one and it's always crowded there. I go there very early in the morning, but not this morning."

As I wiped my face with my hand, I could see a disturbed look in her eyes. Then she stamped her foot.

"What's wrong?" I asked.

"You didn't ask me why I didn't go to the well this morning."

"Why didn't you go?"

She pointed at the empty pail. "Where do you get the water from?"

"From that well. The landlord, he always leaves a pailful on the table. Every morning."

"You want another pail, chú?"

"Um, yes. I'm thinking of washing myself. It's getting hot."

"Try the pump. See if you can get any water."

I laughed. At first she just looked at me, sullen. Then she laughed a small, clear laugh. I said, "Guess I can't wash myself until we get the electricity back, eh? Such a shame they don't have a winch for the well. If you can't use the electric pump during the outage, you can haul water by hand with a crank. Next time bring a bucket and I'll get you water from the well here to take home.

No wait."

"Why are you so kind, chú?"

Her sourness piqued me. "Haven't you been around nice people?" The tone of my voice caused her to avert her eyes, then her lips curled into a cynical smile.

"You guessed wrong, chú. People here are nice. Daddy is nice, very nice."

"And Mom?"

She gave me a dark look. "Just Daddy," she said finally.

"What about Mom?"

She heaved, disturbed. Her eyelashes batted.

"Where is she?" I asked. "Daddy said never talk about her. Said he doesn't know her."

The way she rushed the words kept me from asking any more questions. I glanced at the empty pail, then up at her. "Guess I'll be heading into town later on. At least they have electricity there."

"It'll be back on before evening, chú. Around here, nobody likes even days."

"Now I know. I'd better stock up on water and wash myself on odd days then."

She unknotted her kerchief and knotted it again. It fluttered in the breeze, which was now coming in steadily from the sea. "I must get going," she said, opening the safety pin on the front pocket of her blouse. She took out a wad of money in rolled-up bills and counted them. Nodding, she stuffed them back into her pocket and fastened it with the pin. "I'm going to the market. You want anything there, chú?"

"Why are you so kind?"

"Chú!" She stomped her foot.

"Can you get me two packs of cigarettes?" I took out my wallet. "I wonder if …"

"They have the kind of cigarettes you smoke, chú."

"How d'you know what kind I smoke?"

"I saw the pack."

I placed the money in her hand. "Do you cook?"

She didn't answer as she carefully added my bills to her bundle of cash. Her long, tapered fingers had dirt under the nails, some bitten down. At the inn she ran errands, cleaned the lodge. But cooking? She had a stick-thin body. A child, or rather a teenager, or perhaps a woman already. She was fastening the safety pin, smoothing the front of her blouse. I couldn't help noticing the teensy shapes of her breasts. She lifted her eyes with a provocative gleam.

"I cook, chú. Are you surprised? I cook for Daddy."

"You have time?"

"I make time stand still."

"Really?"

"When Daddy comes home from the sea he's too tired. He's out to sea before sunrise, back at sunset. Well, you know how long each day is for a fisherman, chú?"

"I'm beginning to know."

"I help the woman owner here during the day. I take care of Daddy in the evening."

"Where is Mom?" I asked again.

"She's not with us."

The girl crossed the back court, passed the well, and slipped down the dirt path overgrown with cogon grass so tall it hid her from view, then she reappeared walking on the sand where patches of spider flowers bloomed yellow. Her figure grew smaller as she crossed the pumpkin patch, the pumpkins bright orange against the glare of white sand.

five

"The sight of red country figs always mesmerizes me," Miss Phượng told me. We were standing in front of her house watching a bee crawl into a fig through a round opening at its tip. After a moment the bee's hind legs appeared as it backed out of the fig. With a twist it turned and flew off.

Miss Phượng watched the bee's flight. Long lashes shaded her eyes. Her curly hair shone in the sun as I looked at her face. Then she dropped her gaze.

Just as with her helping girl, I could not tell her age.

"Auntie," I said to her.

She looked up at me.

I opened my wallet and showed her a photocopied cutout of a black-and-white photograph.

"Me?" She smiled.

"When was this taken?"

She pursed her lips. Faint wrinkles crowded around her mouth. "It could've been around the time my father passed away. How did you come to have it?"

I told her I clipped it from a magazine. She had no memory of what I'd told her before.

"What article?" she said. For a moment she gazed at the newspaper clipping. Then she motioned for me to wait. She returned with a photograph framed in antique silver. "My father," she said.

He was a mammoth of a man, sitting solemnly on the edge of a blackwood divan, the long rear panel of his glossy green brocade robe swept under him, draping the divan. The seat was high, yet his feet were firmly on the floor. Next to him she stood like a little girl. His hair was white, thin on top and pulled into a chignon at the nape of his neck. His hands rested on his thighs; his nails curved like talons.

She said the photograph was taken in their old house. In his final years, a civilian after sixty-three years of serving the royal families, he had been sightless, blinded by cataracts.

She sat down on the rim of the rock basin in the center of the courtyard. A dragonfly flitted on the water, causing a tiny ripple. She'd told me they had a rock basin like this one in the old house in which she and her father had lived. The rock basin on which she was sitting was built in his memory.

"That afternoon when I came back from school," she said, "I was crying. My father was sitting on the rim of the rock basin. He raised my chin with his finger and asked me why. The naughty kids at school, I told him. I told him that, as I was peeling the sweet potato he'd packed for me, a girl in the class saw it, gathered other girls around me, and sang:

The half-caste eats sweet potatoes, ho ho!
Without skin,
But when she eats dog meat she spares
No skin, no hair, heh heh!"

'You're half Vietnamese, half French,' my father said. He then held me in his arms. 'Let your teacher know they've offended you. Half-caste is a bad word.'

"I told him, 'You never speak of my mother. Did she die?' I could feel his hesitation. Then he said, 'Phượng, when I left the imperial palace, I wanted to have a child, so I went to an orphanage in Huế and found you among newborn babies.' In a soothing voice he explained about orphanages and why newborn babies were found there.

Then he said, 'I don't know anything about your parents other than their nationality. But I am your father.'"

* * *

At times when she was herself, she could, at her leisure, repaint her past with ease. Places where she'd taken me would come back to life, and the memories that haunted them, like a swath of sun-bleached fabric long forgotten, trembled with sounds and smells.

A week after I first met her we took a trip to Upper Đinh Xuân, the inland village that lay sixteen kilometers from the seaside. She grew up in Upper Đinh Xuân with her foster father, a former grand eunuch of the Imperial Court of Huế. The villagers called him Sir Bộ because of the benefits awarded his own birth village in the deep south, by the Mekong River, when he was formally chosen by the Ministry of Rites.

To everyone who asked about her, her father told the same story: that he adopted her as a newborn from an orphanage in Huế. His neighbors adored the little girl whose dark brown hair was curly with a soft sheen. Many women loved to touch the little girl's nose. Then they laughed and giggled as they compared their own, short and flat, to hers. Pink and white bougainvillea dotted her village, and a dirt path hemmed by hedges of bear's breeches led to her father's house. A flame tree stood outside the house. Year-round shade, as old as the earth. The loose foliage cast shifting light on the ground and in its broken shade the little girl would stop and pick up a scarlet cluster of flowers. Her father named her for the flame tree's flowers. Phượng, a bright fire.

* * *

The summer heat often drove her and her father outside onto the steps of their house, where they'd sit sharing a bowl of rice. One such evening, when she was four, the air filled with the sawing of many locust wings. The sky was dark and bloated as the insects swarmed through the village. People ran out of their houses, some still holding rice bowls, some with toothpicks stuck in their teeth, some carrying toddlers astride their hips, all watching the sky. Phượng hid in the house, frightened by the sounds of their wings.

Night fell and the locusts still buzzed. They crashed against the window shutters like pebbles thrown by little rascals. She couldn't sleep. Her father soothed her as the locusts detonated against the house.

That night she dreamed of a little girl standing by their pond. She stood, drenched, looking at Phượng. The girl's eyes were beautiful in their tranquility. Long, curly lashes shading them. When Phượng woke, it was dawn. The air was quiet. She thought of the locusts, relieved they were finally gone, then thought of her dream. It shook her, it was so real.

She opened the door and went to the lotus pond with the girl's face still fresh in her mind. She stood in the exact spot where the girl had been, where old green moss coated the rim of the pond. In her pajamas, with dreams still clouding her eyes, she waited for something nameless. When she turned to look down into the pond, her foot slid on the moss and she splashed into the water, and started sinking.

All she saw then was her father, bright amid a long dark tunnel of water that made no sound. Breathless, she sensed that she had lost him forever.

Just as everything collapsed in a black shroud, she felt a hand grab her.

After her father had dried her, he sat her down and looked into her eyes, frowning.

"Phượng," he said soothingly, "what were you doing by the pond at this hour?"

"I wanted to see the girl."

"Little one, I didn't see anyone out there."

"I was scared last night. The girl came to be with me." Phượng glanced toward the pond. "She left to go to the water."

Her father nodded. "You saw her by the pond?"

"Yes."

"What did the little girl look like?"

Phượng pointed at her chest. "Like me. But it's not me. She's someone else."

He held her hands in his. "Dear, you were dreaming."

"I wasn't dreaming, Father, I saw her."

He leaned down and touched his forehead to hers. "Don't ever go to the pond, unless I'm there with you."

* * *

People in the village knew her as the eunuch's daughter. She was different from the other children. As we spoke, her eyes strained to piece together fragments of her childhood, of the secret of her birth. Then she would mesmerize me as she pulled out memories, one by one, from the dark womb of her past. Time pinpointed. An early spring day in 1954. She was twelve.

* * *

That night, before bedtime, Bộ sat reading a newspaper he had picked up at the communal house. On the wall beside his bed hung a map of Vietnam. The valley of Điện Biên Phủ, four hundred and thirty kilometers west of Hanoi toward the Laotian border, was a tiny dot. The small valley in the fog and rain of the northwestern forest foreboded the imminent defeat of the surrounded French army. If the news was true, who would rule the country next? The nationalists were no match for the Communists. If the Communists won, would they pay his pension?

Phượng's voice startled him. "What are you looking at, Father?"

"Nothing," Bộ said sharply, then softened his tone. "It's the fate of our country. Something that will affect our lives." He told her about the besieged French army.

"Our teacher talked about it today," she said. "He said the French were doomed."

"He's a Việt Minh sympathizer," Bộ said. He warned her not to talk negatively about the Việt Minh at school, because she could put him in jeopardy with the local government. "Did you write down what I told you about the emperor's dining protocol for your school assignment?"

"I don't need to. I remember what you told me."

At age twelve, Phượng had an excellent memory. She was to deliver an oral discourse to the class on the emperor's dining protocol, a subject she chose with confidence, given her father's long tenure at court.

Bộ closed the curtains to his sleeping quarters and told her to get ready for bed. Phượng turned toward him. "You told me every Vietnamese name has a meaning. What does Điện Biên Phủ mean?"

Bộ scratched his head. "It means a staunch border

county. You want to be the best in everything, but the head can only hold so much information for one night. Keep your mind fresh and go to bed."

Phượng went into her bedroom. As Bộ dimmed the oil lamp, she came back to his bed. She stood in her shadow against the mosquito net.

"What is it?" Bộ said.

"How can the emperor eat thirty dishes by himself? For each meal? And three meals a day?"

Bộ parted the netting and closed the panels behind him. "Well, my dear, it may seem like a lot. But every condiment is a dish."

Phượng wasn't content with just facts. He had told her that the imperial kitchen had a staff of more than thirty, each in charge of a single dish. "Was he fat, Father?"

"No. Despite the extravagant menus, he was a light eater."

"Who prepared his meals?"

"The Culinary Hall prepared the food. The food was stored in gilded-red lacquer containers, and a team of porters carrying parasols took the containers to the palace."

"Who served the emperor? You, Father?"

Bộ was pleased by the question. "No, my dear, the emperor had his own attendants. Is that all?"

"Yes, that's all."

"You forgot the kind of rice they served him."

"I forgot the rice." Phượng smiled. "What kind of rice was it?"

"Try to remember. It's still there in your mind."

* * *

The next day when she came home in the afternoon, her father was sitting on the doorstep, drying his hair in the sun. Each time she saw his long hair she thought he looked like a wizened old woman with a huge man's body. He was reading parched, yellowed documents, and across his knees lay a long ivory bamboo tube, carved with flowers in red and yellow and lavender.

She knelt before him on the cement floor. The sunlight yellowed the paper scribbled with faded black letters. "What are you reading?"

"Documents from the court," he said, rubbing his eyes. He rolled up the opaque sheet and slid it carefully back into the bamboo tube. "I keep all the important documents in this tube. Documents about money and government pensions and the ownership of our house and property. You'll find it behind the altar. When I die, you'll know what to do."

She could smell the light, fresh scent of honey locust lingering in his hair, recently washed in the dark concoction of the dried fruit boiled in water.

"If you die," she said, "who will raise me?"

"I've thought about that. When that happens, you can move to the Temple of Guanyin and live there until you're an adult. The abbot will arrange for the sale of the house, or you can return to it when you are older. He will provide you with shelter and education on my behalf." Deftly her father twisted his hair into a knot. He never used a hairpin to hold his chignon in place. "Do you want to live in the temple if I die?"

"I know no one there."

"Sometimes one has to start all over again in life." Her father's voice was calm. "I hope you understand that."

"I'm not afraid. I know you'll protect me from the

otherworld."

But what had he told her about the otherworld? When she said that, he cupped his large hands around hers, making them disappear. He said in his soul he didn't fear dying, but he feared the hardship his death would bring her. He gazed at the *phượng* flower in her hair and, after some musing, removed it. She saw tiny day-old wrinkles in its petals.

"Father, can a eunuch have children?"

"No, he can't."

"Why can't he?"

"Because eunuchs are males who were born without sexual organs."

"Is that why you couldn't have children?"

Her father grinned. "Did you do well with your presentation today?"

"Yes, but they laughed at me."

"Did you talk about the rice served to the emperor? Or did they laugh because you got it mixed up?"

"No. It came back to me. The town of An Cựu supplied the best quality rice grains. The imperial kitchen picked each grain and cooked the rice in a small clay pot made in the village of Phước Tích. The kitchen used a rice pot only once, one for every meal."

"But they laughed at you? Why?"

"Our teacher was very impressed with my presentation. He asked who helped me. I told him in front of the class that my father was the former grand eunuch of the court." She looked down at his gnarled hands. "At recess some of the kids yelled at me, 'Daughter of a eunuch? That's a miracle!' They said other things too."

"Let your teacher handle it," her father said. "Don't react to them. That only goads them into more harassment."

"They always come around, Father. I was upset, but I didn't cry. Oh, you know something else? I thought how little I know about you." She sat down beside her father with her satchel between her knees. "That's all I've thought of today. I know so little about why you adopted me. Why?"

"I was old and I never had a family of my own."

"Were you lonely?"

He put his arm around her.

"But why did you choose me?" she said. "Why not a pure Vietnamese baby?"

"Because … you looked like someone I once knew."

"Who?"

"Ân-Phi."

"The concubine?"

"Yes."

"How well did you know her?"

"I used to serve her. I was the grand eunuch for six-ty-three years."

"What is a grand eunuch?"

"A grand eunuch is the head of the imperial servants."

"How long did you serve her, Father?"

"Nearly twenty years."

"Was she as old as you when she died?"

"No, she died young, only in her thirties." Her father felt around in his cloth belt. "She gave me a gift once. I have it here."

He put a phoenix pendant in her hand. "When you're older, you can have it all the time if you wish."

She held the ruby-red gem before her eyes. "Beauti-ful," she said, her voice trailing.

"So was she, my dear. Beautiful to behold, and in spirit."

"Why did she give it to you?"

"Because I tended to her during her years as a concubine."

"How did Ân-Phi become a concubine?"

"Her father offered her, his only daughter then fifteen years old, to the next-to-last Nguyen emperor. Not just anyone could do that. Her father, Sir Đông Các, was one of the four supreme Mandarins of the Huế Court."

She asked what the concubines dressed like, and he told her: red, green, and blue. Silk, satin, and sometimes cotton. Never black or gold.

"And what about you, Father? What color was your dress?"

"Green for the senior eunuchs, and blue for the junior." He paused. His eyes had a faraway look. "Phượng," he said finally, "Do you know why the concubines were forbidden to wear black or gold?"

"Why?"

"Because gold was for the emperor and black is the death color."

"But Ân-Phi would have looked majestic in black."

He puckered his lips and thought for a moment before asking why.

"Because she must've had very beautiful skin, like me," she answered.

"She had beautiful eyes too, like you."

"Why did you adore Ân-Phi, Father? Did you love her like you love me?"

"I don't know. But if someone were to take you away from me, I'd wither like a mummy."

"I want to be with you always. How did she die?"

"She went mad after she became a civilian. She used to give her jewels to the poor on the street in her insanity.

No one knows how she died."

"Mad?" Phượng's eyes opened wide, then another thought occurred to her: "You didn't wither after she died, Father, but you'd wither without me?"

He told her when Ân-Phi's death came so suddenly and without warning that he felt something like a shock that left him numb. The numbness, he said, however hard, eased with time, which as Heaven intends, heals every mortal wound.

In his silence she caressed the flowers etched on the bamboo tube and said, "The people at the orphanage didn't tell you who gave me up?"

"They wouldn't do that. It's confidential."

"What about *your* family? Will I ever meet them?"

He told her where he came from—in the deep South, by the Mekong River—and how the anomaly of his sex made him a candidate for the palace. "The court sent for me when I was ten," he said. "Took weeks by sea, and many days by river." He told her that when he became the third-ranking palace eunuch, his father was exempted from labor tax for the rest of his life. He said his parents visited twice when he was still young. "The distance was so great back then, and I wasn't allowed to return to my birthplace once I became a palace eunuch."

Hearing that, she rested her head against his side. "How awful to be alone, Father," she said with a deep sigh.

He held her in his arms. She could feel him trembling.

* * *

She told me about the concubine, Ân-Phi. Her father routinely traveled to the village cemetery in Gia Linh to pay homage to Ân-Phi. After the war there was no one to tend to Ân-Phi's tomb. Men and women had followed one another to the "new world" in Cochinchina, where they found work on the French-owned rubber planta- tions; others headed for the coal mines in Tonkin. So her father took it upon himself to be the custodian. On those trips he carried Phượng on his back as they traveled by ferry to Gia Linh. Every few months he bought white pebbles in jute bags to replace any around her tomb that went yellow. Other times he filled chinks in the masonry walls or on the headstone with mortar, and during rainy seasons he scooped muddy water from waterlogged holes dug by wild dogs and rodents, and then refilled them.

During his many visits, she watched her father, solemn in his green brocade robe, walking around the tomb to inspect the weatherworn stone wall. Bedded with white gravel, the tomb sat below tall, swaying cypresses. He wore his palace garb only once or twice a year, always with an ivory tablet hanging on his chest. Once she played with it and saw that its smooth surface was inscribed with Chinese characters. He said they told his name and rank during his tenure in the Imperial Court.

The incense he burned at the grave sent spirals of gray smoke drifting in the breeze. He placed a bundle of yellow bananas, a few mangoes and pomegranates on a dish beneath the incense holder, then stood in front of the headstone and bowed three times.

Phượng knelt by the headstone, reading the epitaph. She made out the words "Quỳnh Hương, Ân-Phi."

"Father, you never told me – what is a concubine?"

"A concubine is an emperor's wife, but she's not the queen. Our emperors used to have many wives."

Phượng examined the names on the headstone. At

eight, she could read both French and Vietnamese, but some of the Vietnamese words on the headstone were beyond her grasp. "Is Quỳnh Hương her name?"

Her father squatted and dabbed her brow and cheeks with his handkerchief. "That was her name before she became a concubine," he said. "It means princess flower."

"So she was named after a flower, like me?"

Her father smiled. "Yes. And then she became Ân-Phi. That was her concubine title." He folded the handkerchief away. "Every concubine had a title."

Phượng became familiar with the birds that nested in the trees in the cemetery. On hot summer days she would hear cuckoos in the boxwood and bear's breeches, and her father told her he remembered the sounds back in the old days at the Palace Eunuch Hall, the lazy, throaty sounds that made one drowsy. A few times she spotted a family of crested mynas building their nest on a very tall tulip tree and, as she lay nestled in his lap, he told her how Canh, a young eunuch once under his care, used to tell him that mynas kept their dwellings out of human sight. Her father said Ân-Phi would be pleased to have such wondrous life around her. There were wagtails and starlings and kingfishers. As she watched them, each kind to its own special tree, her father recalled that Ân-Phi once told him that it was their instinct for safety that made them do such a thing.

One day she saw a flock of parrots descending from the sky to perch on the poon trees around the concubine's tomb. It was noon and the earth around Ân-Phi's tomb – her father had bought the finest soil to build the foundation – was bright yellow in the sun. The sky was soon full of the rustling of wings as another flock of parrots came screeching to join the first. Soon the trees were full of them, red-beaked and black-beaked, crackling the air with their cries. In one deafening rush of wings, the birds swooped to the ground and started pecking at the yellow soil as if they were catching earthworms she could not see. But to her astonishment they were eating the yellow dirt, not insects, devouring it with a manic delight. Dust dulled their plumage, and soon one bird looked just like another. The white pebbles were no longer white, but yellow, like the headstone and the surrounding walls.

Her father ran into the sea of birds, shooing them away with his conical hat. In a loud whoosh, the parrots took to the air. Just as he threw his hat at them, they descended to the ground again and resumed pecking at the yellow dirt. Soon so many were eating in a frenzy that the ground was a canvas of colors – red, blue, and green, all dusted in a yellow haze. Her father didn't know how to deter them. She yelled to him, "Throw rocks at them, Father!" But he shook his head firmly, said, "That would upset Ân-Phi. She'd share all that was hers with the world's creatures."

Her father felt guilty for failing to keep Ân-Phi's tomb sacrosanct. At home, all night he pondered the parrots and their behavior. Why did the birds ravage her tomb? Was Ân-Phi under some curse? Or was her spirit trying to communicate with him through the parrots?

Soon after, father and daughter boarded the ferry to Gia Linh to inspect the damage. There were older people like her father on the ferry, and he struck up a conversation with them about the birds at the tomb. An old man smoking a hand-rolled cigarette told him the yellow dirt was used to pack around coffins for burial. He said there had to be something in the finest yellow dirt the parrots needed to cure themselves of a certain disease, the same way dogs chew certain leaves until they throw up to rid themselves of a sickness.

Her father didn't know what to believe, but he thought of refilling the ground with clay to buy peace of mind, and then on second thought decided to use yellow dirt again to see if the birds would come back. Was it soil they craved, or was it a sign he needed to heed?

Her father made several trips to the cemetery pushing a cart piled high with bags of the finest quality yellow dirt. While she scampered after butterflies fluttering among the graves, he filled the depressions around the tomb with yellow dirt. He finished late in the afternoon. Dusty and tired, he sat under the cypress as he had before, and waited.

At sunset, she lay resting across his lap. She saw the crested mynas returning to their nest on the tulip tree, but no parrots. At dusk they went home, but returned to Gia Linh the following morning. He took a seat beside Ân-Phi's tomb and watched the sky. No parrots, red-beaked or black, returned.

* * *

Inside the house she took me to a room that had only a bamboo cot, a low table on which lay a teapot, two tiny blue-on-white teacups, a pair of fine long brushes, and a writing tablet in jade green. "My father's parapher-nalia," she said, touching the teapot with her fingertips. Then she lifted a handle-less porcelain teacup, small as a plum, its rim banded with gold. She raised the empty cup between thumb and forefinger, sipped, peering over its rim at me.

"You know," she said, "I never overslept in those days

when I was still working, because my father never over-slept. At dawn I'd wake to the bitter scent of tea in the air, and find him sitting in the main room like a giant statue by the glimmer of dying coals. Once he joked, 'You'll oversleep the morning I die.' Then he told me the story of a butcher who lived by a pagoda. Every day before dawn, the monk in the pagoda chanted the morning *sutra*, and the butcher would wake and start his day by slaughtering a pig. One morning the monk was sick and skipped the *sutra*. The butcher overslept. When he woke and got ready to kill a sow, she was giving birth to a litter of ten."

"So did you oversleep?" I said. "After he died?"

She didn't answer. She sat down on the cot and ran her hand along its yellowed, smooth edge. It was a long cot, the kind rarely seen in Vietnam. "This is his cot," she said softly, as if her father were due back soon.

"You must have loved him very much, Auntie."

I realized how redundant my words were.

"My father," she said, "had known and touched many things in his life. Yet nothing made him feel more attached to this world than this cot."

I looked at her, at the bed's smooth bamboo, and felt the man's presence.

He was just a boy, she said, the first night he lay on this cot, trying to fall asleep in a strange place far from home. He was neither boy nor girl and his village saw his going as a benediction. Because of his service, the village was exempted from labor excises for several years. His father told him that he should be grateful to serve the emperor – the divine representative on earth, who maintained the harmonious balance between Earth and Heaven. Palace service would bring him that much closer to the divine.

"Not many villages are blessed with a boy like you," his father said. "A boy born without the burden of sex, his thoughts are clean. That's why the Imperial Court of Huế values boys like you. Be proud, son, because you have brought blessings to our village."

But her father knew that being sexless was more burden than blessing.

The ten-year-old southern boy cried when the ferry pulled away from the landing, leaving his father a mere silhouette on the dock, and didn't stop until the boat reached Huế.

Later, much later, when he reached adulthood, he thought somebody's prescience gave him such a long cot. By then he stood six feet five inches tall, taller than all the Frenchmen who came to the Huế Imperial Court. But that first night in the Palace Eunuch Hall he slept on this long cot, alone, in a dark room, and cried. An old eunuch came in and gave him a tubular pillow. The pillow, with its fresh smell of linen, bore an old scent from home.

* * *

In that age-old eunuch system, emperors came and emperors went. Her father served each one, and in time witnessed the royal burial of each. He served each emperor's high-ranking concubines, and saw them introduced at the age of fifteen to the emperor, watched them grow into womanhood, then old and feeble. His fellow eunuchs looked after the aged concubines in the Peaceful Hall outside the Purple Forbidden City until their last day. Some of the concubines, still in blossoming womanhood, were exiled to the emperor's necropolis when he died. There, they lived out their lives tending to his tomb.

One of the imperial concubines her father served came from Gia Linh village, Quỳnh Hương. Her royal title was Ân-Phi and she was the second-ranking concubine of the nine rankings. When the emperor died in 1925, many people from the Gia Linh village believed that, with her noble lineage, she would become the next queen mother. Because of Đông Các's stature in the imperial court, his daughter was made a third-ranking concubine, and then elevated to second-ranking within three years.

By then the emperor had many wives, yet his bedmate was a male attendant. The emperor never touched Ân-Phi as one of his wives and she bore him no child. Frail with bone marrow cancer and often sick, the emperor needed care even after defecation. A low-ranking eunuch would wipe him with a piece of gold silk, then another. His penis, small as a child's, could have qualified him to be a palace eunuch.

* * *

Among all the concubines, Miss Phượng told me, the aristocratic second-ranking Ân-Phi had impeccable manners and beauty, which suited her to be the next queen mother. But the emperor's will decreed that the only wife who had given him a son would be the next queen mother, even though she did not have the same pedigree. After the eight-year observation of the emperor's death, the coronation of the queen mother was to take place that year: 1933.

Miss Phượng said her father told her only once about the coronation of the queen mother.

* * *

On coronation day Bộ got up early.

Under the stone bridge the lotus pond mirrored a blue sky. A propitious day, according to the court astrologers, to crown the queen mother.

Bộ walked through courtyards under the shades of white-flowering poon and frangipani trees. Curving tile roofs, glazed yellow and blue, loomed into view behind green foliage, then disappeared from sight. Mourning doves cooed in the cloistered courts and flower gardens lay quiet, green in the sun. But, on this day of grandiose enthronement, he felt detached. He wondered how Ân-Phi felt.

The queen mother to be crowned did not have a respectable pedigree. The deceased emperor met her when he was still a prince who loved gambling. She conceived a child and implicated the prince in her pregnancy. The prince's mother, knowing her son's sexual incapacity, had her interrogated. They dug a shallow opening in the ground, made her lie face down with her protruding belly secured in the aperture, and beat her. Though she and her unborn baby survived the beating, the child's paternity was never revealed. The prince claimed the child was his. Without an heir, the French would never have enthroned him. He made the woman his queen.

For eight years after the emperor's death, Bộ had noticed the woman's changes. The future queen mother became more and more isolated as if to distance herself from her peers. She kept her feelings to herself, no longer congenial during Ân-Phi's visits. After those visits, what came to Bộ's mind was the beauty of friendship ruined by egoism. The futility of grandeur.

Bộ once asked Ân-Phi what she thought of the queen mother to be. Smiling, Ân-Phi told the grand eunuch, "Bộ, a person never changes at heart. It comforts me to know that. You must be wondering why, yes? Because in my heart I know she's lost, befuddled. I wish I could help her. Do you think she stops reminiscing the many times we concubines used to share our thoughts, our jokes, our laughs like the most carefree creatures in the world?"

At night Ân-Phi played the piano, some nights Schubert, some nights Chopin. Bộ asked her one night, "Ân-Phi, if it is true that I can gauge your mood by the melody, then am I wrong in expecting to hear melancholy in the music you play?"

"You're not wrong, Bộ. It's just because I'm not in a pensive mood tonight – or on those nights when I happened to play."

"Ân-Phi, your music is always blithe, always merry."

She could read his unasked question, for the grand eunuch with his good heart and intention had occasionally let his wishes be known. For eight years, he had carried a wish as if for her. As if in light of the situation, she was withering inside for losing the queen mother's crown. That night, after hearing her answer, Bộ told her in a hushed voice that he admired her noble spirit and doubted that she would fall victim to some mad aspiration, such as becoming the next queen mother. "Ân-Phi," he said, "you are caring, spontaneous, and so humble I wonder how you have survived among the sharp tongues and mean spirits in the palace."

By midmorning that day Bộ received news that the emperor's son, enthroned eight years before at age twelve, was on his way to the Palace of Diên Tho, the new queen mother's residence. He hurried across the courtyard and entered the palace. The somber interior was cool in the summer, warm in the winter. He bowed to the queen mother. "Your Highness," he said, "it is time."

Ladies-in-waiting surrounded her, arranging the folds of her robe. The queen mother closed her eyes as one girl placed the crown on her head. The crown was elaborately embroidered with nine phoenixes – symbol of fidelity and obedience, and the imperial supremacy of the empress – and filaments crusted with sparkling beads of ruby, pearls, and red corals falling from its sides. The queen mother bloomed from homely to splendid.

Bộ led the way across the reception hall. The queen mother minced in her golden knitted slippers with phoenixes on their tips, glittering with ruby dust. Even with two attendants on either side of her, she carried the weight of the imperial robe of magnificent richness like an octogenarian groping her way without a cane. How many weavers and dressmakers had touched the golden brocade?

Once on the throne behind a velvety curtain that hid her from view, she sat still in her robe. Its front was stitched with an enormous Chinese character: Longevity. Beneath her robe she wore a hand-sewn gown of blood-red silk. The queen mother remained frozen, her face so sickly pale that her father felt not pity but empathy for the chosen. *Be yourself and be thankful to those who rendered their service to you.* With one final look at the queen mother to be and the female courtiers who stood at attention on either side of the throne, Bộ withdrew.

* * *

The French Resident – the representative of France and ruler of the country – and various dignitaries arrived, greeted by court ministers at the Palace Grand Gate. The hall hushed. The silence fell on the crowd of Mandarins and royal families and soldiers. Floating music rose in the distance from the Grand Palace, drifting from out of the open back doors. Slowly it drew nearer and nearer until one could hear the languid notes of a melancholy chord coming back again and again. The heralds pronounced the arrival of the emperor. Their voices echoed from the rear of the palace, relayed in succession from behind doors of long dark halls, on the open terraces, the winding corridors through which His Majesty must pass.

As the emperor sat down in the Main Hall, the French Resident proceeded across the floor of gleaming blue tiles until he came to stand in front of the throne on which the queen mother sat. His solemn voice echoing, the French Resident commenced the ceremony with a speech of good wishes. He recalled His Majesty's father's ascent to the throne, seventeen years earlier, reminiscing about that auspicious day in which he was honored to partake, and expressing his deep gratitude to the Huế Court for recognizing his attention to His Majesty's father's service then, and his diligence to the court now.

Looking at the queen mother's face, Bộ felt the woman's agony. She sat shrunken in her enormous ceremonious robe, her face flaxen, her small hands protruding from the long loose sleeves gripping the arms of her throne. Her soft black eyes darted from side to side as if she dared not make eye contact with her well-wisher. Her slightly thick lips in pale red rouge drooped at the corners, and Bộ could tell tension had sapped the queen mother.

Now in his bright yellow grand court robe, tied with a jade belt and a headdress carved with nine dragons vying for a pearl, the emperor came to kneel in front of his mother, folding his arms across his chest. In his monotonous Vietnamese, he offered his mother his best wishes and his accolade for the French recognition of her coronation. While he remained on his knees, a white-bearded Mandarin translated the emperor's words into French.

Bộ dabbed his face with a folded handkerchief. Relieved, he let out a sigh as the melodrama was about to end for the queen mother. Bộ watched the Minister of Rites lead the royals to the enormous mat before the throne where they prostrated themselves, ten rows deep, rising and falling five times to the queen mother. Out in the sunbaked courtyard, imperial guards with yellow leggings ported long rifles with fixed bayonets, keeping order among rows of Mandarins in flowered robes, who knelt on tiny mats, kowtowing in harmony with the prostrations inside.

Even from inside the hall, Bộ could hear the booming voice of the commanding French officer shouting orders, and native imperial guards set off strings of firecrackers fluttering on bamboo poles from the four corners of the courtyard. In the deafening noise, Bộ moved among servers in the hall, watching them serve ice-cold champagne and cakes and sweetmeats. French guests peered up at the huge grand eunuch who moved nimbly behind other eunuchs with high cheekbones, directing them to different spots in the hall.

By noon the ceremony was over. The royal orchestra played a farewell concert, and the high-pitched sounds of indigenous musical instruments rose clinking in the air.

As the emperor's entourage passed through the Palace Grand Gate, the Great Cannon fired three rounds. The ground shook. Bộ walked down the veranda, directing his staff to line everyone up according to rank and role. The human line shifted, merged, wrapped around the eastern and western verandas of the pavilion. Noon heat shimmered on the *yin-yang* tile roofs, and white glare scorched the ground.

Ân-Phi stood under a huge pink parasol. The lady-in-waiting assigned to her was a new girl who had taken the place of Ân-Phi's old faithful attendant, who had recently died. The wizened woman had spent three months to recover from her illness in Peaceful Hall across from the Palace Eunuch Hall. Then, shortly after returning to Ân-Phi's side, she died. They brought her body over the northwestern wall to be taken away for burial, and Ân-Phi and Bộ stood among her attendants watching her being hoisted with a winch and disappearing behind the high wall.

Now flashes of red, blue, and yellow caught the eunuch's eyes. The queen mother, surrounded by ladies-in-waiting, was on her way back to her chamber.

Bộ shouted, "Kneel! Kowtow five times!"

The line dropped. Fabric rustled. "Rise!" Bộ roared.

The line rose: bearers of incense burners dressed in aqua blue, fan bearers in sea blue, and parasol bearers in royal blue. A sea of parasols shifted, bright, colorful. Huge fans flapped. Clouds of incense misted the sky, smelling of embalmed wood. After the queen mother passed by, Bộ surveyed the line of well-wishers. His gaze fell upon Ân-Phi. Had fate favored her, she would have been the object of all the accolades, all the prostrations.

A ruby earring at Ân-Phi's feet caught Bộ 's eyes. After the concubine gave him permission, he tenderly affixed the gem to her lobe.

"Ân-Phi," he said, "aren't you glad that it's over?"

"Bộ, I'm glad that it's over," Ân-Phi said, smiling. "So is the queen mother."

* * *

I often wondered if someone like her father, a born eunuch, could fall in love with a woman like Ân-Phi.

When I asked her such questions, Miss Phượng told me age never played itself into her father's life with Ân-Phi. His love for her was asexual. Miss Phượng was amazed at how time could not purge that delicate love, neither possessed nor possessing, and the only reason for its timelessness she knew was that it sprang in response to the concubine's transcendent beauty.

Miss Phượng passed me this image. By a lotus pond stood the concubine watching the maids pluck the lotus seedpods, her hair draped over her shoulder in one long, black swath. Her body curved gracefully; one shoulder dipped slightly. Her eyelids drooped in a gentle curve, pensive and serene.

Then, while I listened in silence, Miss Phượng slipped into a reverie. She relived his memories with a rare deliberate evocation of his first encounter with the concubine.

* * *

On the solemn day of her royal wedding, Ân-Phi arrived in a carriage drawn by four white horses outside the Trinh Minh Palace, home of the second- and third-ranking concubines. Bộ didn't see the concubine's face as she stepped down from the carriage holding a giant brocade fan in front of her. He stood beneath the portico observing the cortege escorting the new bride to the Throne Room where His Majesty was waiting. Two female courtiers, each holding a pink parasol, flanked her. Behind her, walking in pairs, trailed female porters carrying wicker-white snow geese, drooping willow twigs, long and fluttering, and lacquered coffers so black the white of the attendants' dresses hurt his eyes. Ân-Phi and her entourage followed the two female attendants, each with a paper lantern in her hand. As they entered the deep shadow of the portico, the lanterns glowed in brighter orange.

The eunuch gazed at the bride. Lively figures of dragon and phoenix hugging the moon were embroidered on her long vermilion robe, on her slippers. Each step her delicate feet took was accompanied by the tinkling music of her earrings and bracelets, encrusted with figures of nine phoenixes. As she drew near, he straightened his back, then stood absolutely still. When he glimpsed her face, his heart stirred.

Ever since Ân-Phi's introduction into the palace, Bộ tried never to lose sight of the concubine. He said, once, that to see her was to know what heaven meant by beauty.

* * *

On the afternoon after the wedding, Ân-Phi's tired feet brought her back to her reception chamber. She sat while a female attendant prepared tea. The girl went about her business as silently as a shadow, her feet seeming to glide, and she lifted and replaced objects with the lightest touch, as if the clink of porcelain on wood would shatter her lady's nerves.

When the attendant, her eyes downcast, brought tea

on a red-lacquered tray, Ân-Phi inclined her head and the girl set the tray down soundlessly. Just as Ân-Phi was about to speak to her, the girl bowed and half-lifted her gaze. "We have an hour until lunch," she said. "Ân-Phi, please rest if you are tired." A warm whiff of incense came from her clothes as she bent to pick up a footstool and place it in front of the armchair. "Please rest your feet, Ân-Phi."

Gently she lifted the concubine's feet, still in jeweled slippers, onto the footstool. She served the bride a cup of chrysanthemum tea and as she put down the teapot, Ân-Phi spoke to her. "Thank you, Miss. You may now excuse yourself until I need you again. I'd like to have a moment for myself."

Ân-Phi, finally alone, looked around. The room was like a strange face peering at her, the solitary visitor. Yellow roses on the tea table drooped from a porcelain vase in a profusion of blooms, permeating the air with their scent, which clung to her skin, her clothes, her hair. The morning was spent, and the midday sun shone intensely through the stained-glass window, brushing shadows into the chamber corners like cobwebs.

A faint taste of wine from her toast with His Majesty lingered on her tongue. During the ceremony she had glimpsed the sickly sallowness of his face, the receding chin, the birdlike fragility so effeminate that, enhanced by the sparkling gold crown and enormous diamond rings on his fingers, His Majesty resembled an aging dowager.

She sipped her tea, soothingly fragrant, but felt languor rather than comfort. She had no idea what the day would bring, nor what the night would hold. A highly organized person always in charge of her life, she now felt lost in a labyrinth. Where would she find the map of her new life? Did she want to see it? At the thought, exhaustion seized her. When she woke, she didn't know where she was, until the bright light from the stained-glass window caught her eyes, and the scent of roses made her wonder if she had been embalmed in her sleep.

A huge man in a shimmering green brocade robe standing beside her, like a tree, startled her. Hardly moving his head or lips, he said mildly, "Lady Ân-Phi, I am Bộ, the grand eunuch. I am honored to be at your service."

"Please be seated, Mr. Bộ." She motioned toward a rosewood armchair across the tea table.

"Please call me Bộ, and allow me to remain where I am in due respect to you, Ân-Phi."

She couldn't tell his age, though his hair, tightly woven and tucked under a black hat, looked pale gray. His large, deep eyes focused on space, never meeting hers. She asked why no one had told what was expected of her as the newly inducted concubine, save for a flurry of instructions before the ceremony.

Knitting his eyebrows, Bộ told her that he could not brief her on the protocol upon arrival because there was not enough time before the ceremony. In a soft, steady voice the eunuch explained what she could expect of her attendants—the tea must be served in a tiny cup while it was still hot; the rice must be served warm in a small bowl; and tea and rice must be refilled immediately the moment her attendants spotted them empty. Bộ paused and pointed to a pear-shaped silver bell hanging by the door: whenever she wished to summon them, day or night, she should simply sound the bell.

"Why are they so passive in my attendance?" Ân-Phi asked.

Bộ tipped his head slightly, as if to gauge her meaning. Though she understood their silence was part of
royal protocol, she believed people should be allowed to
behave more openly and reciprocally, within reasonable
bounds. She said the moment one became an automaton,
the air everyone breathes and shares would be tainted
and even flowers – she cast her glance at the abundant
yellow roses – would wilt before their time.

Bộ clasped his large hands before him. The fingernails
arched downward in opaque white. Then he said, "They
are not to ask, but rather to obey orders, Ân-Phi. The
hundred-and-twenty-year-old protocol of the imperial
court has been and shall be observed. Such is tradition.
In light of your view, however, one can only surmise that
protocol, being circumstantial at best, can be rewritten in
favor of a certain monarchic rule, or, Heaven knows, the
colonial rule. Only time will tell."

Then Bộ inquired about her wellbeing and explained
the wedding ceremony to be followed with its strict etiquette, the afternoon appointments with the queen and
each of the royal concubines, and then the evening.

When the eunuch did not mention her wedding
night, Ân-Phi asked calmly what arrangement he had
in mind for her. He coughed a tiny cough and, with a
quick glance toward her, said that His Majesty's health
was everyone's concern for the time being, and therefore the nuptial night would have to be deferred – he
paused with a nod – which was not unusual considering
the monarch's ongoing illness.

Ân-Phi kept her composure at the news. Before she
left home her mother had whispered to her, "When His
Majesty heard your father's offer to betroth his daughter to him, he said, 'My palace is a monastery. It shall

be your discretionary decision whether or not to turn your nubile daughter into a nun by bringing her here.'"
Ân-Phi had locked this revelation in her heart.

After a sip of tea, Ân-Phi regarded the grand eunuch with equanimity and told him she expected to be briefed fully about her role as the third-ranking concubine. At her calm voice, Bộ bowed and said none of her attendants except him might brief her on the subject of protocol, which would come in due time. His mission was to be her chief attendant, that should she make any mistake regarding etiquette and decorum, the error would be his and his only because of his failure to prepare her. That said, he asked softly if she wished for anything. "A book," she said smiling.

When Bộ turned toward the door she thought he was leaving, but he stopped at the lectern and returned with a book. He placed it next to her tea, silently, as if noises were sins. Astounded, she looked at the title of the book, *Les Misérables*, and peered up at the eunuch, joy spreading across her face.

"Is it coincidence or serendipity that you picked this?" she said. "It's my favorite book."

"It *is* your book, Ân-Phi," Bộ said, stepping back.

During the nuptial ceremony he had asked her parents about her hobbies and then personally sorted through her book collection which, together with her other belongings, was being kept in a storage room pending one final examination of Ân-Phi's possessions to verify that everything was intact.

Bộ stood with his back to the lighted window, one hand cupping the other, and spoke of what she was perhaps expecting above all else. Her grand piano. It would arrive soon, he said, coming by ferry and then by cart.

Just before he left, Bộ bent over the tea table, and tested the warmth of the tiny teapot. Then, with a crisp motion he refilled her cup and bid her farewell. The mass of his body, softened by the fluttering panels of his robe, stirred the scent of chrysanthemum tea.

* * *

That night, Ân-Phi couldn't sleep.

The gong of first watch sounded from the watch tower. She listened to its echo trailing a soothing note. When it faded she sucked the back of her hand. In the scent of her own flesh, the scent of her mother came to her. She sat up. Perhaps she could read, as she did on wakeful nights at home. But her book was on the tea table in the reception chamber, and she didn't want to disturb the attendant who slept there.

She paced the room in the dark, hearing the tiny creaks of the hardwood floor under her bare feet, the fresh scent of her nightwear lingering in the air. Back and forth she paced, hoping the lump of homesickness would leave her throat and the weight on her chest would subside.

She heard a tap on the door and her attendant appeared, holding an oil lamp in one hand and a long round pillow in the other. "Ân-Phi, since you can't sleep," the girl said, "perhaps you would like to see if this pillow would help."

A fragrance of grapefruit flowers came from the satin pillow as she took it from the attendant, who said the pillow came from Bộ, to be given to Lady Ân-Phi should she have a sleepless night.

So Bộ had also asked her parents about her favorite

flower. In truth she loved many flowers, but as dazzling as roses were, their scent lacked the eternal captivation of the grapefruit blossom. That was a little secret she shared only with her mother.

She lay down, hugging the pillow. The scent hung frail in the chamber.

six

I stood in the narrow doorway of their small hut, watching the helping girl clean her father's infected toe. He had passed out. "Drunk," she said. Every evening.

Twilight. The briny air was warm. Voices of the sea in the distance − the sound of crashing waves, the sibilant winds hissing through the dune grass, a sudden cry of a shore bird.

She picked up a canvas bag and slung it over her shoulder. "I must fix Daddy's net."

Outside, dusk was falling. Her red kerchief looked darker.

"Which way to the wharf?" I asked.

"This way's shorter, chú."

"I never noticed the shrimp ponds around here."

"I don't like seeing them."

"Why?"

"I hate them."

"Because they pollute the water?"

Her lips crimped, she shook her head.

"Don't you care?" I asked. "Those pesticides and chemical wastes from shrimp farms?"

"No." She threw me a mean sidelong glance. "I live here, chú, I know."

"But you don't care?"

"Chú!"

She must have also known that beyond the seaside, toward inland, shrimp farms had encroached the mangrove forests where fish and other marine life live and spawn, the forests for centuries protecting the inland from tidal waves, from wicked storms.

"Daddy said there are so many dead fish in the ocean now. Chemical wastes from those shrimp farms kill them." She paused, then in a dead tone said, "Daddy will kill those shrimpers. He will."

I glanced at her. Her face looked serious. I never told her the purpose of my visit to Vietnam. That I was to write my thesis on Vietnam's environmental degradation caused by shrimp aquaculture. Twenty years after the war. Half a million hectares of coastal mangrove forests had been razed to become prawn farms to feed the American market.

Moral advice percolated in my head, but not a word left my mouth. I knew nothing about their lives here. Going down the foredune there was a tang of fish odor, a damp smell of kelp in the air. Fishing nets were piled up above the high-tide mark and beneath them lay the ocean litter of seaweed, soggy sticks, bits of crabs' claws. High tide was coming in, tinkling softly through the orphaned seashells studding the sand. I stopped when something scurried out from under the mass of wet nets. A rat. She followed its trail and said the bad rat was out looking for birds' eggs, those that nested above the high-tide line. A buoy clanged. A desolate sound guiding fishermen ashore.

Her father's boat rested on the sand among others, its bow leaning down on a pair of wooden stakes. A net draped its length, spreading over the sand. Above the water the wharf shone bluish under the iron lanterns, and in their pale illuminations she inspected the net, hooking her fingers in the twines of the rips, her brow creased.

"Fresh tears?" I asked her.

She scratched her head, then said, "I hadn't had time to fix them," as she swung her bag down and dropped it on the sand.

"Anything I can do for you?"

"I can do this faster on my own. You'll get in my way if you help, chú."

I asked if it took long. She looked at me, tilting back her head. "I wish you could fix a net just once and see what that'd do to your back after hours sitting on your knees."

"And how much do you get paid?"

She shook her head sadly, said, "Chú, different sizes different fees," then pointing at the worn-looking net, "that net is about the length of five arm stretches, I got fifteen thousand *đồng* to fix the rips and recrimp the leads."

"A dollar," I said.

"It isn't much where you come from, chú."

I said nothing, just looking at her headscarf, now a bruised red, the light blue of her short-sleeved blouse that hugged her scrawny body, the copper-tan of her skin, the long fingers that held the scissors as she snipped off the loose tag ends, cutting them off here and there all the way to the knots of each mesh. She did this quickly, cleanly.

I asked if she'd throw away the net damaged by a sizable hole. She put away the mending needle as if she didn't hear me, and then slowly she began removing the guiding twine that had been threaded through the meshes. Finally, without looking up, she spoke. "You never throw away a net, chú. It's like throwing away money."

"Okay then," I said. Annoyed by her quirky mood, I decided not to ask what she or her father would do with such a damaged net.

"Don't you want to know how I'd fix a large hole, chú?" She turned to me, her arms akimbo.

"Yes, I do."

"I'll patch it. It takes much longer to patch it." She saw my quizzical expression and shrugged. "It's hard for me to explain. You must see it, chú. Like you first trim the hole into a square. Then you cut out a patch from a scrap net, its edges must match the edges of the hole so when you lay the patch in, it fits. Then you can weave."

"How often did you have to do that?"

"A few times. Takes a whole evening."

"Out here by yourself?"

"Yes, chú."

I nodded. Something dark inside me made my words sink back. Not pity, but helplessness. Had she, this woman-child, ever gone to school? Had she the time to rest? What did she dream when she slept?

"Would you like to go to school?" I asked before thinking it through.

"Yes, chú." Her quiet tone surprised me. "I hope someday I will be able to." She started looping the guiding twine around the mending needle and then tossed them into the bag. She spoke into the bag. "Auntie" – she meant Miss Phượng – "wanted to raise me and put me through school. But Daddy wouldn't allow that."

"I see. Well, he can't do much without you …" *Useless ass!* I stopped before those words left my lips.

"She loves me like her own daughter."

"But she doesn't have a daughter."

"No, chú. How could she? She never married!"

I chuckled at her clarity. "Do you love her like you love your mom?"

Her eyes suddenly narrowed like a cat's eyes. "I don't love her," she said.

"Who?"

"Mom."

"And why's that?"

She picked up her bag and slung it over her shoulder.

We walked back up the dune, stepping over clumps of brown seaweed, our feet kicking up sand, sending sand fleas flitting across the sand. Then her voice came. "Mom ran off. She lives with a shrimper now."

seven

From behind a dune dense with filao trees, Miss Phượng's house looked toward the sea. The evening was windy, and the wind stripped filao cones from the trees and they fell like hail on her roof. In the lull, the sound of falling cones stayed with me.

On the veranda, Miss Phượng picked up a cone the size of an acorn. "Do you have these in America?" She put the cone in my palm.

"I don't know," I said, rolling it with my fingers. It felt spiny with its woody sharp scales colored reddish brown like cockroaches.

"They make for prickly walking," she said.

I took the teacup and its saucer and stood as she lowered herself onto the glider. Then, feeling awkward, I perched on the railing. It was dim where she sat, but the glow from the lamp inside shimmered over her face, white against her hair.

Miss Phượng never wore lipstick or mascara. She didn't need to, for, at her age, she still had the wholesomeness of a cold-climate fruit like a red apple. In a beige blouse and a moss-green skirt, she looked as fresh as the white cups of Queen Anne's lace that dotted America's roadsides.

"May I ask you a personal question?"

"Yes, Minh."

"Are you French or Vietnamese in your soul?"

"I am both."

As I smiled, she said, "Jonathan once asked me something like that."

"Jonathan?" I said. "Oh, Jonathan Edward, who died in the cane field." The Viet Cong believed he was CIA, she had once told me. They stopped him on his way to visit her one evening and killed him.

"He said to me, *Est-ce que vous êtes une française qui parle vietnamien, ou une vietnamienne qui parle français?* Because he spoke French very well. He could speak Vietnamese too, though not as well as French. *Je suis les deux,* I told him."

"So, which of your parents is French? What happened to your real parents?"

"I didn't know who they were. Even my foster father said he didn't know. For years. Would you like another cup?"

"If you don't mind, Auntie."

She went back inside. I gazed at the dune. The high wind had torn down the staked tomatoes and the ground was now scattered with fruits and leaves. A fruit bat might pick up the smell and eat the fallen tomatoes. She came out. I received my fresh cup of tea. "Thank you, Auntie."

She offered me a bar of chocolate.

"This is French chocolate," she said. "Not as sweet as American chocolate, that's my warning."

I didn't know how light it was until it melted in my mouth. She was right. I preferred the sweet Hershey chocolate. "It tastes … quite different," I said. The hot tea nearly scalded my tongue. Over the years, she told me, foreign journalists, writers, mostly French, had sought from her stories told by her father about life in the Purple Forbidden City. They came with gifts.

"Can I ask you another personal question?"

"As long as it's not about French chocolate, which you might not like."

I smiled at her guess. "Did you find out who your real parents were?"

She came to the railing, standing a few feet from me, and faced the sea. After a while she spoke.

"I often asked myself that question when I saw people worship their deceased parents on the altar. Who are my parents? Where did they come from? Then I stopped asking."

"Why's that, Auntie?"

She wrapped up what was left of her chocolate bar. "My foster father was a dignified civil servant. I was afraid …"

Suddenly I understood. I looked into her deep-set

eyes. Those western eyes held my gaze briefly, then blinked. She was brought up by a respectable man. Dignity and decorum. I thought about the Indochina War, the French soldiers who raped or slept with native girls. There was a silence.

"You aren't afraid anymore to inquire about the truth?" I broke the silence.

"In my heart," she said, "I was dying to know who my natural parents were. But having been abandoned at an orphanage, I didn't have the heart to know who that baby's parents were."

I drank my tea. "Auntie," I said, "Would it matter who you were supposed to be?"

"Who I am today," she said, smacking her lips, "isn't complete without knowing who I was supposed to be." Then holding up the pendant that always hung below her clavicle, she said, "This ruby phoenix has something to do with my birth. When my father gave it to me, he told me Ân-Phi gave it to him. When I was older, I learned that this ornament wasn't carved as a pendant. I believed that the gem had been cut into two equal halves, and one of its halves is with me."

She worked the chain off her neck and dropped the pendant in my hand. A piece of ruby, its back flat and smooth. She had worn it since childhood, and it wasn't until she was eighteen that she discovered that it wasn't meant to be worn as a pendant. On gemstones pendants, she explained, the animal carvings were small and flat. Her phoenix was three-dimensional—the bird's long, ribbony plumes and crests, dance-like and real-looking with its tail feathers and wings. Its taut curved lines, its varying depths were the result of complex handicraft, rare achievements that only could have come from the hand of a master sculptor.

"It all began with this pendant," she said once again palming the ruby. "But really it began with Jonathan Edward."

I leaned my head to one side, staring at the stone's mellow shine. "Will you tell me more about this Jonathan Edward, Auntie?"

"Jonathan Edward," she repeated the name. Silence, then, "He was with the Agency for International Development. And his reason for studying Vietnamese was to help himself deal with South Vietnamese officials in developing a Vietnamese civil administration. He said, 'We want to win the people's hearts and minds and bring the boys home. But before that can happen, we have to earn the trust of the South Vietnamese officials. If they don't speak English, then we must learn their language.'"

She smiled to herself then said, "I still feel the earnestness in his voice. He had a gentle, deep voice like you."

I smiled and asked, "So he was with the much maligned AID pacification program."

"Yes. They must repeat the French pacification program in Vietnam. Except not fail. And you know what he said? He said it helps if you speak the language because then the Vietnamese will treat you like a member of their family."

It caught me off balance. "Who told him that?"

"The Pentagon."

"Well," I said, shaking my head, "you might befriend a Vietnamese quicker if you speak to him in his mother tongue. But I don't know if he'd treat you like a member of his family."

"Me neither," she said.

I was so close to her I could feel the thumping of my heart as she told me of their first meeting.

* * *

They met on a late summer morning.

She was standing at the stove in her noodle shop. A young monk came in and asked her if she wouldn't mind coming out to meet someone. He led her out of the shop, and she looked at his companion, an American.

"She is his daughter," the monk said in English to his friend.

After a moment of hesitation, the American mustered a faltering, "*Chào cô,*" a flash of pallor dimming his complexion for a second. His gaze never left her face.

She sensed his self-consciousness. "Hello," she said in her mother tongue. "Do you really speak Vietnamese?"

"Please, don't laugh, Miss. My Vietnamese is bad."

"Why are you looking for my father?"

"Mr. Bộ is your father, Miss?"

"Yes, he is."

She touched the rims under her eyes, moist with perspiration from the cooking heat and the sun.

"I wish to see him," he said.

"What is this about?"

"This is Minh Tánh," he said, without taking his eyes off her, "my guide from the Guanyin Temple, and I'm Jonathan Edward."

Then in his hesitant Vietnamese he said he was looking for his lover's parents. Françoise was a Vietnamese-French girl, he said. It was here in the hamlet of Upper Đinh Xuân in 1944 that she was found as a baby, floating down a river. She had with her two photographs.

They showed a thatch-roofed house with a lotus pond. He took a deep breath and said, "I just learned that your father lived in the house around that time."

She looked at the American, mesmerized by his tale. As she listened, something stirred in her. She thought of the little girl who had come to her in her childhood dreams, that time by the pond when she fell in to see her and almost drowned.

"Where is she – your Françoise?" she asked the American.

"She was raised in North Vietnam," he said. "Her foster father was a Việt Minh cadre. She went to live in Lyon in France until she graduated from university. I met her in Washington, D.C., where she taught Vietnamese to me and other men from U.S. government agencies."

Breathless, he paused to get his wind. Then he said, "She died" – his voice shook – "recently."

Phượng looked up at him. "As soon as my customers leave, I'll take you to my father."

"Thank you," he said. "I'm terribly sorry for disrupting your business. And one more thing." He paused. "May I ask for your name, Miss?"

She smiled. "Phượng."

* * *

She walked fast, shouldering two oversize copper pots bobbing on a shoulder pole. When Jonathan offered to help, she told him she was used to the weight, that she left home at six-thirty every morning with two fully loaded pots. He asked how she could shoulder such a load back and forth every day. He didn't know that nothing is hard once it becomes routine. He asked her how far she lived from the market. She said it was about four kilometers and the cross-village bus seldom ran her route.

At times he became lost, and she had to repeat what she had said. At times she was lost because of his accent. Sweat dripped down his face. It must be from the sun on his neck, from anxiety about the language. Though the day was hot, she wasn't tired. Her cheeks, her forehead perspired but lightly. The young monk trailed behind them, looking weary and glum.

"Does your father speak French, Miss?" Jonathan asked her.

"Certainly." She looked up, dabbing her forehead with the heel of her hand. "I speak French too, if you want to speak French."

Jonathan glanced back at the monk and so did she. Sweat beaded the monk's pate and brow. It seemed every time she looked back she saw the monk's gaze on her.

"Sure," Jonathan said in French. "I wish I could explain how much it'd mean to me to discover the truth of Françoise's birth."

Their shadows moved ahead of them.

In his silence she imagined his lover standing before her just like the little girl of her dream.

The road curved around a field, a world of green sugarcane leaves. Low thatch-roofed houses sat back from the road; their doors propped open with sticks. After a long while on many dirt paths, she turned a corner. They entered a cobbled courtyard, the stones churning loosely under their feet. A masonry screen fronted the house. At the base of the screen lay a basin of rockwork, and in it a still pond.

She lowered her load onto the ground and entered the house, stopping momentarily outside the pleated curtain leading to her father's sleeping quarters. She parted the fabric just as her father opened his eyes, closed and opened them again. Though he could no longer see because of cataracts, he knew the sound of her clogs.

"Why are you back so early, Phượng?" he asked hoarsely.

"Father," she said, sitting down on the cot, "I bring you a guest. An American wants to see you."

Her father winced.

"What happened, Father? Why are you sleeping now? Don't you feel well?"

"No, I haven't felt well since last night. I have a recurring pain in my stomach." He raised himself up with an effort. The cot creaked. "What does he need from me?"

"He wants to find the origins of a baby girl. He believes that she was born in our old house in Upper Đinh Xuân." She stopped when she looked at the paleness of her father's face. Then she went on, "What is this all about, Father?"

With a wave of his hand, he rose from the cot. "That's what I would like to find out too. Would you show him in?"

She seated the guests at a wooden table facing the pleated curtain. Her father emerged, a giant shuffling one step at a time to the center of the room. Out of respect for his guests, her father had put on his eunuch's robe. His lime-white hair was thin on top, rolled and tucked into a chignon at the nape of his neck. He stared in front of him as his hand felt the rounded corner of the divan.

Jonathan and Minh Tánh rose to greet him.

"Comment allez-vous, Monsieur?" Jonathan asked, gazing up at the host.

Her father tipped his head. "May I ask who this is?"

"My name is Jonathan Edward."

The monk did not speak. Her father set his eyes toward him. "And who is it there?"

"My name is Minh Tánh. I'm a novice at the Temple of Guanyin."

Her father gestured formally toward the chairs. "Please be seated."

He stood until they were seated and then sat gingerly on the corner of the divan, sweeping the long rear-panel green silk under him, letting it drape the divan. Then he turned to the guests, resting his hands on his thighs. His fingernails curved like hooked claws. In a soft voice he asked her to serve the guests. She turned and went to the other end of the room, through a doorway hung with a pale blue curtain. She returned with a tray and two glasses, and set them down on the table.

"Please have some sugarcane juice, gentlemen," she said.

The monk drank the frothy yellow juice in one swig, set the glass down and burped. Jonathan sipped it and then leaned to the monk.

"I wish to speak to him privately."

Her father whispered to her. She rose and Minh Tánh, almost tumbling over his own feet, followed her outside.

* * *

Alone with the guest, Bộ sat erect like an old bamboo tree.

"Sir," Jonathan said, "do you mind if I speak to you in French?"

"Certainly, Jonathan." Bộ pronounced the guest's

name with the French *oh*.

"Sir, I hope my sudden appearance at your door doesn't intrude too heavily in the privacy of your home. I'm thankful to your daughter, who closed her business at midday to bring me here to see you. I come here today on a mission for a girl I love. It has to do with her mysterious birth. She was lost as a baby, and someone rescued her from a river in the hamlet of Upper Đinh Xuân."

Bộ, blind, couldn't tell his guest's age from his voice. Though deep, a softness around its edge made the speaker sound innocent and youthful. His French was accent-free. Bộ felt he was being transported back to colonial days, when he was the grand eunuch of the Imperial Court of Huế, routinely entertaining French guests.

"I gather that this friend of yours is Vietnamese?" Bộ said.

"She came from France, but I believe she was born in Vietnam. There are some facts about her birth we can glean from photographs, and I'd like to show them to you." An awkward silence. Then Jonathan continued. "Pardon me for saying that; I was naive."

"Tell me about them then."

Jonathan described the photographs. "There are handwritten words on the back," he said. *"Hamlet of Upper Đinh Xuân, 1942."*

Bộ said nothing and showed no emotion, sitting like an oracle who spoke only when asked.

"I couldn't find any house that had a pond in the hamlet of Upper Đinh Xuân," Jonathan said. "But I was told there was a house with a pond like that back in the 1940s." He paused. "I learned that the original owner was a eunuch. This is as far as I could get in my search."

Bộ's lips parted, but no words came out. In the silence

he could hear voices talking outside. He unlaced his hands and placed one on top of the other.

"How old is this lady friend of yours?"

"She was my age. Maybe a year or two younger."

"Did you say she *was*?"

Jonathan coughed. "She died, Sir."

Bộ's brow furrowed. "There was a question I asked you. I'm going to ask you again. Is she Vietnamese?"

"She's half Vietnamese."

"Half?"

"Yes, half. Do you care to know about her mixed blood?"

Bộ tipped his face and set his sightless eyes on the guest. "Yes, I would like to know."

"She's half Vietnamese, half French. And another thing I haven't told you …"

"Yes?"

"She could pass for your daughter."

Bộ pursed his lips. "Do you mean she looked like my daughter?"

"She looked exactly like your daughter."

Bộ shook his head. "How could it be?"

"I don't know, Sir."

"Does she have a name, Jonathan?"

"Françoise," he said. "Her name is Françoise."

Bộ muffled a groan.

Years before, when he had to travel to Lower Đinh Xuân, he would ride a ferry, even after the main bridge was rebuilt in Upper Đinh Xuân. Each time he ferried downriver, he saw the silhouette of the bridge in the rain, and at night he would dream that he stood on the bridge while a little girl stood on the rain-washed riverbank watching him intently. She always stood in the same spot as if waiting for him to claim her, but each time he was cemented to the bridge, unable to reach her.

He lowered his head and placed his hands on his thighs. Jonathan broke the silence. "There's something that belonged to her that I wish to give to her family."

Bộ didn't lift his head. "Go on," he said finally.

"There's a ruby phoenix that she used to wear around her neck. She said it'd been with her since her birth. My job is to find her family and give it back to them."

"Didn't she have any relative in France?"

"She had her foster parents. They both died."

"Who were they?"

"They were from North Vietnam and worked for the North Vietnamese government."

Bộ nodded and said nothing.

"She then lived with another family," Jonathan said, "that became her second foster family."

"Yes?"

"French missionaries. They were close friends of her Vietnamese foster parents."

"You said you had a …"

"A ruby phoenix. A pendant."

"Do you have it with you?"

"Yes."

Bộ received a leather pouch in his hands and slipped his bony fingers inside. He felt the pendant; his lips parted slightly, and after a while he pulled the drawstring shut and extended his hand toward Jonathan. His palm remained open for a moment as if it didn't feel the pouch being lifted, and then his fingers curled in slowly, his hand shaking.

"This is where I am, Sir," Jonathan said.

Bộ looked down into his lap. "When did she pass

away?"

"About eight months ago."

"What did she die of?"

"In a car accident, Sir."

"Please tell me about the car accident."

"What is it that you wish to know, Sir?"

"I wish to know how it happened."

"She was in my car with me and it crashed into the rear end of a lumber truck. She died without a head."

Bộ heard a clink in the quiet. Jonathan must have set his glass down.

"How is she related to you, Sir?"

Bộ lowered his head. "She's not related to me."

"Sir?"

Bộ didn't answer.

"How can this be?" Jonathan said.

"Strange as it may seem, I don't know her."

"Despite all the facts – "

"I realize the facts."

"But so many facts line up; she could be your daughter's twin sister – pardon me for my unwanted supposition – are you sure she cannot be related to you, Sir?"

"She's not related to me, Jonathan. That's one more thing you must realize."

"Please help me," Jonathan said, his voice strained.

Bộ, sightlessly staring at him, said nothing.

"It wasn't her wish to trace her origins," Jonathan said. "It wasn't her wish at all."

"Why wasn't it?"

"She didn't want to face some reality she could live without."

"I speculate that she'd been reared in a respectable family."

"Since she was a baby."

"Since she was a baby," Bộ said.

"They found her floating down a river in a basket. She was just an infant."

"Who were they?"

"The people who later became her foster parents."

"Whereabouts did they find her?"

"I don't know. Somewhere in this province."

Bộ muffled a sigh. "Do you believe in fate? Jonathan?"

"Only if it means something I must accept because I can't change its outcome."

Bộ listened, clasping his hands in front of his chest. Then he turned his opaque eyes toward Jonathan and said, "You and I both believe in fate, for it means exactly what you said – there are things we must accept because we can't change their outcome."

eight

Miss Phượng's memories were fragile. At times they were like the blue in the sky, that throbbing blue you could touch, feel. Other times they were fleeting shadows. Chase them, and they flit like fish at the bottom of a creek.

On this hot afternoon, the taxi we rode in bounced on the rutted road, red dust hazing the air. We were coming back from the Citadel where her father had lived for sixty some years. I asked the driver to take us to Upper Đinh Xuân, where Miss Phượng had lived for most of her life. She asked why, and I said, "I want to see it through your eyes."

"Through my eyes?" She touched her sunglasses, smiling. "Do you trust them?"

"Absolutely."

I felt warm deep down. Now she looked blank, her hands folded in her lap, gazing out, and I realized she must be tired.

When we passed the cane field, she looked back and asked, "Do you have a childhood friend – not just any childhood friend, you know what I mean?" "No," I replied, and she said, "Mine died in that cane field." The name of Jonathan Edward came to my lips. But a childhood friend? I surmised that it wasn't him when she spoke again, "If one day they take away the cane field, perhaps to turn it into a giant shrimp farm, I'm afraid I might lose my memories forever."

The taxi was going down a winding road paved with cobbles in coral pink; the shade of the trees made it cool. We passed an open-air market, the cab moving slowly now, and there were people gathering at the entrance, the sun beaming on their ivory conical hats. She pointed toward the market. "That's Well Market," she said. "There used to be a public well nearby that gave the market its name. My old noodle shop is still there. I sold it."

"After twenty-some years?" I asked.

"Yes. My father bought me a stall at Well Market when I turned sixteen. It was empty, so I had to furnish it with tables and chairs. Six tables, twelve people would be a full house. He warned me that I would have to stay up late every night making rice noodles for the next day and get up at five in the morning to make the broth and then shoulder two copper pots to Well Market. From a tiny stall it grew into a large beef noodle shop. Twenty tables, small and big, which seat up to fifty people."

"Why selling noodles, Auntie?"

"My father asked the same question. I told him I wanted to learn a trade I could be proud of and get rich with it. He said, 'You'll forfeit your schooling? You know you can continue your schooling and be carefree. When you go into business, you'll no longer be carefree. You'll deal with profit and loss, with an eye toward growth and gain.' I said, 'I've been thinking of what you told me would happen if you died while I was still young. I want to do the right thing.' He finally consented. He said at sixteen I had blossomed into a girl who would attract men, so he hoped I wouldn't become a peddler wandering the streets. He'd rather not see me going on foot from place to place, which could be dangerous. I said to him, 'The concubine you served, Ân-Phi, if she had been born poor like me, with an old father like you, what would she have done?'"

She paused. I glanced at her. Wasn't the concubine's eminence the sum of her pedigree and beauty? What would have become of her had she been born poor?

Then, after a long silence, Miss Phượng spoke. "My father said, 'Ân-Phi would have done what was best for her family. Now if you live in Gia Linh, the most respectable trade is rice noodles. The Gia Linh clan has owned that for over a century, and they supply noodles to all the beef noodle soup vendors in the Thừa Thiên province. The recipe can never be copied. The Gia Linh clan keeps its formula a family secret. They never hire labor from outside. Do you want to learn such an art?' I thought for a moment, then said, 'Would they teach me if that means competition? Why don't I go into the beef noodle soup business instead of making noodles?'"

Before I could ask if she had a talent for it, Miss Phượng smiled and touched her brow with the palm of her hand. "I remember now," she said, "there was a street vendor who passed through our alley every day selling hot beef noodle soup around the time I'd come home from school. She made the best broth. Just to hear her old scratchy voice crying *Beef noodle soup!* made my mouth water. I asked her how she made the broth, and she just looked at me. I wrote down her recipe while she stared at my scribbles. I was fourteen when I made beef noodle soup the first time, and my father said, 'Dear, someday you'd make the best of all.' I remembered those words."

Miss Phượng looked toward the market, the din hammering our ears. I followed her gaze and saw an old woman with glass vials and cups, sitting at a lamppost with another woman whose shirt was pulled up to her shoulder blades, revealing pale white skin. The old medicine woman dropped some liquid into a glass cup and lit a match. A flame spurted inside the cup. She stuck its mouth against the woman's back. As she let go, the cup stayed in place, sucked onto the woman's flesh. Three other women waiting their turn squatted in front of the patient.

Turning away from the window she said, "My father told me then I could make rice noodles for my beef noodle soup business. That'd help avoid direct competition with the Gia Linh clan. He said, 'Let's agree on one thing. You dedicate yourself to the soup trade, and I will stand behind you in good and bad times.'"

nine

Twilight. On the side of the foredunes, sheltered by tall hedgerows of vetiver grass, the sandpipers rested. An early mist hung pale over the wharf and the waves broke in empty booms against the wharf's pilings, and the buoys clanged.

The helping girl wasn't alone by her daddy's boat. A man was coming towards her, and she backed away, jabbing the mending needle at him. I ran across the sand. She turned around to pull on the net and he lunged for her from behind and pulled down her pants. I stumbled and regained my footing and saw her swing around, her arm flying across the man's face. She saw me and quickly pulled up her pants.

He was an old man. Dropping down on the sand, he cupped the side of his face with his hand. I stood over him. A small, sharp-cheekboned, gaunt-looking man. His sweat-stained brown shirt had holes on the front like cigarette burns. The wind blew sand in my face. I could smell his unwashed body tinged with alcohol.

"You leave her alone," I said to him. "Or I'll break every bone in your body."

"Yeah? Ain't done nothin' to her, ain't I?" he slurred in his viscous twang. "And look at what she done to me. Look." He moved his hand off the side of his face. There was a dark red gash from the tip of her mending needle.

I picked up her lantern and brought it close to his face. "You're lucky," I said. "You could've been blind in one eye. Now get lost."

He scrabbled around as if he had lost something. Then his hand came up with a squat-looking bottle. He shook it, then twisted open the cork and sniffed, mutter-ing into the empty bottle as he staggered away. I watched him lick the bottle's neck as he bobbed across the sand and disappeared between the dark hulks of docked boats.

She looked calm as she adjusted her headscarf. "How did you know I'd be out here, chú?"

"I didn't see you at the lodging house. The owner said you didn't come today."

"I was there today. Cooked and washed dishes."

"She said you weren't there. Said you'd probably be out in the pumpkin patch. Were you?"

"I was there yesterday. But not today."

She got paid to help load up the trucks with fresh-ly-harvested pumpkins. Those ripe pumpkins were heavy, their hard rinds in deep orange, hollow sounding when thumped. She said she worked the whole day until her back gave. Then she said, "The inn owner has moments like that. She's got today mixed up with yesterday."

I brushed the sand off my face.

"Don't you have a handkerchief, chú?" she said. "It's very windy tonight."

"I'll bring one next time. Who's that guy? A hobo?"

"You can say that, chú. He's drunk most of the time." She knotted a corner of a mesh with twine and snipped it with her scissors. "One time when I was younger, eleven, twelve, he almost got me good. That evening I was coming down the dune over there to look for Daddy, he jumped out on me from behind a filao tree. Drunk as a skunk. That good-for-nothing old buzzard."

"Then?" I squinted my eyes at her.

"He got my legs locked with his so I couldn't crawl away, and, and …"

"Pulled your pants down?"

"Yes, chú. I threw sand in his face and then I felt something hard in my hand and it was a horseshoe crab shell. It has sharp spines. And then as he bent to try to, to … I hit his face with the crab shell, and he fell off me."

"Did you tell your daddy?"

"Daddy has always known he was crazy, ever since he was a boy. He said, 'Next time just outrun him.' That old drunkard."

I shook my head, told her that if it'd happened in America, he'd have been locked up for good. She said, "Because America is rich." Then asked, "Did you see anything, chú?"

"See what thing?"

"What he did to me."

"Yes. He pulled down your pants." I paused. "And your panties."

"Chú! You saw?"

"Well, you asked me."

"No, you didn't see. Okay?"

"Okay. I didn't."

"Can you help me hold the net down?"

"Certainly."

There was a large rip toward the center of the net, still damp, heavy from seawater and smelling of fish. She'd cut out a patch from some throwaway net and the patch was draped over the gunwale. As she put the patch in place, I said, "Such a big hole. What happened?"

"It was rough out there today," she said. "Daddy didn't go out far. He set the net closer to shore. Lots of sharp rocks near the shore."

I watched her weave. There was a dry sound of wings beating overhead and looking up I saw a lone gull flying out into the darkening, misty ocean. Straggling fishing boats were coming home, bobbing past the buoys toward the wharf where several gulls were already perched on the pilings, waiting. In a moment they would shriek with pleasure when the fishermen hauled up their seines heavy with fish.

It was dark when she finished mending the net. The waves swelled and the wind blew out her lantern. She lit it again, her face suddenly awash in the orange illumination, her eyes a wet brown. I asked her if she'd had dinner. She nodded. Then she opened her canvas bag, rummaging around with her hand, and came up with two packs of cigarettes.

"They finally had them today at the market," she said. "The kind you smoke, chú."

I took the packs from her bony hand and said, "Thank you." Then, as I put the money in her bag, she refusing to take the cash, I said, "I still don't know your name."

"Didn't you ask inn owner?"

"Why can't I ask you?"

"You'll laugh."

"Well. I promise I won't."

She slung the bag over her shoulder and briskly paced across the sand. We moved toward the rows of boats, the sand gritty on my windswept face, and I stopped until she turned around.

"Look," I said, raising my voice, "if you don't tell me your name, I'll make up a name for you."

She stood in one place like a statue, lantern in hand, the sand aglow at her feet. As she turned to head up the beach, she said, "Cam."

Cam. Orange. "Why did you think I'd laugh?" I asked her.

"It's a weird name."

I thought so myself but said nothing. She looked down at her feet, then bent, hovering the lantern over the sand. A ghost crab, tan-colored, was coming out of a burrow, its eyestalks trembling like two black peppercorns as it froze momentarily in the lantern light. Off-white, you couldn't tell it from the sand until it sprinted down the slope.

"Where's he going?" I asked her.

"Follow him, chú," she said, smiling for the first time.

I couldn't see the ghost crab very well, as it had blended with the sand. I watched her pacing in a straight line, the lantern raised high, and soon we stepped onto the damp sand now as dark as the water. Three feet away was the pale crab, barely above the tide line where waves washed in, died, and trailed back. Before I could think, the crab sped backward, farther and farther up the sand flat, turned a sharp angle and stopped in front of a drenched-looking heap of perforated, round-leafed sea lettuce.

"Don't go near him," she said, looking back at me. "He can see you."

"Can he?" I looked again at its round eyestalks. I turned to her and laughed. "I think he is going for a bath."

"Daddy said he needs water to breathe. I mean, the, the ..."

"Air, oxygen?"

"Yes. In the water."

I took a step up and she grabbed my arm. "Don't scare him, chú. Let him get his meal."

"Sea lettuce?"

"No. He eats beach fleas, mole crabs. They hide in those seaweeds."

"I'm going back to the inn."

"I'm going with you."

As we cut across the sand, the crosswind blew out her lantern. She fumbled for the matchbox. In the blackness the sea came heavily on the wind with a wet, briny tang, the hollow booms of waves, and the water glowed in a long swath of light, pulsing like stars. I called out to her. Beyond the wharf, veiled in a white mist, the ocean was ablaze with an electric light of ghostly cold blue, glittering red, and frosty green. She said those were sea lamps. At my exclaimed ignorance she laughed and told me that it was luminescent plankton. I said I wished I could capture the magical sea lamps with a camera.

"You ever seen sea lamps back in America?"

"No. I'm sure they're there. At the right time. I wish I were there."

"With her?"

"My girlfriend?"

"Yes."

"That would be lovely."

"When are you going back, chú?"

I thought, then shrugged. "I don't have a date. Soon though."

"Are you going to marry her?"

I glanced at her. "Why are you interested?"

"I hope you marry her. If you don't, you'll break her heart."

"What if she doesn't want to marry me?"

"You're a man, chú. You can take it."

"Like your dad?"

"Yes. Except he gets drunk to forget her."

"So men aren't tougher than women."

"They are, but women have more to lose."

I smiled, appreciating her honest sensitivity, and carried on walking in the dark by her side.

We walked in silence. After a while, she said, "What's her name?"

"Her name? April."

She said the name to herself. "Do American names have meaning?"

"Some do. Her name does. *Tháng tư*, the month. And it means spring for new life."

"What's she doing in America?"

"She studies, a senior in college." Then, smiling, I shook my head. "She's a student."

"I know she's a student. And what do you do, chú?"

"I'm working on my master's degree. Well, forget that. I'm a student too."

"So you have to go back to school after summer."

"Yes."

She was quiet as we left the dunes. I could smell a strong, musky scent. When I asked her what it was she said nothing. We walked past the pond's shimmering liquid edge, which wrinkled when fish and frogs plopped into it. In the lull I heard peepers and crickets and bullfrogs in the undergrowth.

The musky aroma came back. I sniffled. She said that was the smell of fox and that the creature must be somewhere on the dune. She said sometimes if he is near and if you keep still, you could hear the soft padding of his feet on the filao needles. She knew it was him, a cross fox, his fur smoke-colored, slate-gray down his back and across his shoulders. Sometimes in the evening, when she was out on the beach fixing the net, she'd see him hunting for fish washed up on the shore, or beach rats, which he loved. He ruled the dunes at night. In the early morning you could see his tracks in the sand and, if you followed them, you could understand his habitual itinerary. I asked her how she could tell his tracks from those made by other carnivorous animals. She said, I'll tell you next time. Just come out at first light.

We made it around the marsh, dense now with a heavy fog. Blurred, motionless figures on stilts stirred among the grasses that fringed the pond. The lamplight had spooked the night herons and I could smell their stench on the wind as we walked into the dense atmosphere.

There was no light behind the window shutters of the lodging house. We went up on the veranda and stood listening. "Everyone must be in bed now," I said. We stood apart, like two strangers.

ten

I once asked Miss Phượng, "Do you ever feel French in your soul?"

"I never do," she said.

One morning on revisiting Gia Linh we were walking down an old, paved road. Dogs yapped behind the hedgerows. Two mutts came through a hole in a hedge and sniffed at our legs. Miss Phượng shooed them, and they slunk away. In the morning stillness she said peace was shattered in the summer of 1953, the day war came to Gia Linh. "Right here on this road," she said.

By that year, Miss Phượng said, the fighting between the French and the Việt Minh hadn't affected her village or the vicinity. But it was bad for those hamlets where salt marshes and sand dunes stretched for miles along Route One, the north-south road the French convoys used. The Việt Minh ambushed French convoys and retreated into the hamlets surrounded by swamps and quicksand bogs. The French went after them and bombarded the hamlets or burned them down.

When the Việt Minh began to use Gia Linh as a strategic base, Miss Phượng said, it came under French attack.

"Our house had a dugout," she said. "Many times, my father and I hid in the shelter when French Hellcats came strafing and bombing." He told her that if she got caught in a bombing attack on the road, she should hide in a bamboo grove.

One morning she went to school just as the mist was lifting. She walked under the shade of Indian almond and poon trees, hearing the crows cawing in the trees and in the air. On the roadside stood a small shrine, solemn with its grandiose ceramic tile roof gleaming red, green and white. A group of women fish vendors overtook her, striding up in tandem, carrying rattan baskets in their arms. As they passed, edging her off the road, the stench of dead fish pickled the air.

Then the frantic sounds of drums and gongs swelled. Bombing alert. The roar of airplanes came so quickly, she barely managed to jump into the roadside ditch before explosions shook the earth. The air flamed. The Hellcats swooped, strafing the bamboo groves along the road, leaving a burnt smell behind them.

She dusted herself off, the front of her floral blouse hanging open where a button was missing. "Father!" She ran until her chest ached. Smoke and dust stung her eyes. Corpses lay strewn in the groves. Shreds of flesh and clothing were skewered on branches. She saw her father striding up the road in his gray pajamas, his wrinkled face etched so deep with fright it looked like a mask. His hands shook when he bent to hug her. Cries came from up the road. He took her by the hand and half-walked, half-dragged her in that direction. Past the shrine they saw a haze of dust, the tile roof gone, only the jagged front wall standing. In the smoldering ruins of houses lay the charred bodies of men and women and children. Remnants of fish baskets littered the ground among the sprawled bodies of women who sold fish for a living. She shuddered.

"Why ... did they kill them?" She gasped between sobs.

"They were in the wrong place at the wrong time," her father said tonelessly.

She wiped her tears. "This was their way to the market every day."

Her father squinted at the sun, searching for the long-gone planes that brought death. When he looked down at her, his face was pinched painfully, and his voice dropped. "In wartime a lot of innocent people die. When I said wrong place and wrong time, well, what I meant is fate brought them here where they shouldn't have been."

"But we're not the enemy. Why can't they see that?"

Her father paused to collect himself. "They hate the Việt Minh, and the Việt Minh look like us. When the French can't find the Việt Minh, they'll kill those who share the Việt Minh's skin."

eleven

By the pond behind the dune people came to wash clothes. When it didn't rain for days on end, they fetched water from the pond for cooking and drinking. The helping girl washed her clothes there. I knew clean water was at a premium and told her politely not to use the pond water except to wash clothes. I said that stagnant water gave people pink eye and diarrhea.

At the pond, without soap, she had to wash her soiled laundry twice. She kept checking her rolled-up pants for wetness, carefully wiping her hands with a washcloth, only to soak them again as she scrubbed woolen blankets until her fingertips wrinkled. I'd noticed that a hanging thread on a blouse, a loose shirt button, made her fret. I watched her and shook my head.

"Are you afraid to get wet?" I asked.

She looked at me and back at her hands. "Chú," she said, "you do this when you don't have washers like in America."

She went to the other side of the pond where the water was still and filled the pail with water there. I watched her carry the pail back, plodding along in her new wooden clogs. Most women at the pond walked barefoot. She winced at their cracked heels, at the black lines filled with dirt——her fastidious nature.

"I'll go look for bull nuts, chú."

"What for?"

She puckered her pretty lips, thought for a moment, then turned and walked to one end of the pond where water caltrop grew in abundance. Glossy and black, they looked like a leering goat-horned devil. Folks made necklaces from the dried, oiled nuts, and sold them to tourists.

With a basket of washed clothes under her arm, she walked to the fringe of the pond and carefully left her sabots and the basket on the rim and waded the shallows with her pant legs rolled around her thighs. Ahead of her the surface rippled and something knifed through, heading into the leafy tangles on the pond's edge. "Snake!" I called out to her. "Be careful." She called back to me, "Don't worry, chú, they're water snakes." She went ahead, plucking the pods in a hurry and tossing them into a paper bag. The feathery leaves trembled as the black snake slithered out and cocked its head, watching. She stared at the snake, then hurled a bull nut at it. The snake dipped its head and retreated into the dark mass of diamond-shaped leaves.

"You make necklaces with these? And sell them?" I asked.

"No." She shook her head. "I can't tell you."

twelve

I brought Miss Phượng a grapefruit blossom. "Auntie," I said, "for you." She smelled the flower, closed her eyes, and held still. I watched her twirling the flower on its stem, her eyes gazing at the stamens, mesmerizing dots of bottle green afloat in a wash of white petals. She brought the flower to her nostrils, inhaling deeply. "What is this flower?" she said.

I shook my head in dismay.

Yet she could remember what her father once told her

on the day we went to visit the Palace Eunuch Hall.

We entered the Citadel through the An Hoà Gate, riding past lagoons whose tranquil waters mirrored the blue sky along the northern wall. The ocher paint had peeled completely from the gate of the Palace Eunuch Hall and its name in red on the gate had faded. The defaced stucco walls of the shrine held up the caved-in tile roof. Weeds sprouted in the courtyard. The door to her father's old room was unhinged, and a musty odor and cobwebs hung in spectral gloom. She took me to Canh's room in the east wing, a room vacated by an aged eunuch who had died. The wing housed a water closet and a washroom, and the rest was living quarters with several rooms then vacant, following the abolition of boy eunuchs. As we stood in its emptiness, trying to relive a moment of past companionship, we could hear termites gnawing in the truss. Twelve eunuchs used to live in the hall. A few eunuchs her father's age shared physical characteristics. Their breasts looked like old women's, sagging with dark nipples, and their voices were shrill, unlike her father's, which was resonant. There were a few castrated eunuchs in the palace. When they relieved themselves, they squatted. Her father said they carried with them a quill, wrapped in paper. When they urinated, they pushed the quill into their urethras to relieve themselves like men. Like her father, most of them didn't retire at sixty-five. Since they no longer had families, they chose to serve the royal family until they died.

From there we went to the Purple Forbidden City. As she led me under the moss-covered porticoes arching over the passageway, she said, "This passageway is covered overhead against the rain and the harsh sun, because the emperor walked this way every morning to visit his mother."

She described to me the layout of the three palaces and six halls, the paths that connected them, and, through memory, directed me to places with uncanny accuracy.

"Auntie," I said, "have you forgotten anything at all?"

"I asked my father the same question." Miss Phượng smiled. "He told me, 'I worked my whole life: sixty-three years. I knew every stone, every crack. I knew every smell that changed with the sun's coming and going.'"

In a hall, airy and empty, we stood surrounded by wood-paneled walls painted vermilion, bright with gilt ornaments.

"Where are we, Auntie?"

"Do you see those fan-shaped windows?"

"Yes."

"Trinh Minh Palace, Ân-Phi's former home."

I was struck by the unreality of the vision. This is where the concubine lived. Now we were walking those floors, looking out of those windows. I turned around slowly, absorbing the scene. I imagined the concubine's soft footsteps and her attendants shuffling across the hardwood floor, their low, whispered conversations. Long, undulating robes in red and green and white sweeping the gleaming floor. I pictured her father, wrinkled and old, and envisioned him in his eternal green brocade robe and black hat. She'd told me she loved the hat, which he kept in his clothing trunk. It looked odd with a cicada sewn in yellow thread on the front and with its mouse-tail on the back.

Down a sunlit hallway I could glimpse blue sky through the round openings on the wall. She stopped and felt along the wall with her hand until she touched a door. A clinking chime when she rang a pear-shaped bell.

"This was Ân-Phi's chamber," she said.

We stepped into the softly lit room; the harsh sunlight diffused through a stained-glass window. She set her face toward the window.

"Ân-Phi's piano used to be under the window in this antechamber," she said. "My father told me when you wandered on the walkways and heard the piano, you knew you were near Trinh Minh Palace."

All the adjoining rooms were airy and empty, including Ân-Phi's bedroom. "It's so bare, Auntie," I said. "I wish we could've seen it in the days of glory."

The Purple Forbidden City was conceived and built to obey feng shui laws of perfect harmony between man and the cosmos. Her father said every morning Ân-Phi mingled with other concubines as they walked to the Cân Thành Palace to wish the emperor well. She often visited other concubines, he said, and on such visits her father led the retinue as Ân-Phi reclined on a hammock carried by four men, flanked by ladies-in-waiting holding the accessories for the visit – a pair of slippers, a box of betel and lime, a case of hand-rolled cigarettes. Though Ân-Phi did not smoke, the cigarettes were a courtesy for the host. Some visits lasted into the evening, and on returning to her chamber he walked behind her flanked by two female attendants. Mist hung low on the ground in the dark visitation passageway. Ahead of them flickered the lights of the lanterns the ladies-in-waiting carried chest high. The trembling light emanating like a mist from the globes was yellow, and the only sound was the rustling of her father's robe.

Outside, emptiness and decay seeped through mossy cracks in brick walls, in weedy courtyards where peepers and hares and cuckoos made their homes. I knew we were standing among the ruins of a bygone civilization. She said the only time the palaces looked unkempt in the Nguyen dynasty was in 1849, eighteen years before her father was born. That year a smallpox epidemic killed six hundred thousand people, claiming several lives in the palaces. The emperor fell victim, and though he survived, his face was pockmarked, and he became sexually impotent.

She led me into a garden with a lidded well. As she leaned against its brick rim, she told me about the morning Ân-Phi tried to see herself in the well.

"Canh's spirit had possessed Ân-Phi," Miss Phượng said, "and he wanted to see her in the well."

I remembered the young eunuch, her father's protégé.

As she led me through the garden, she said, "The government has let them fall to ruin after the war. But I can imagine what they looked like. My father said Ân-Phi planted many trees that are still standing in these gardens today. Fruit trees, shade trees, ornamental trees." She paused then said, "Do trees remember who planted them?"

thirteen

Cam hadn't been at the inn for three days.

It was mid-morning when I came to her hut and found her lying wrapped in a blanket on her cot. She said she had bouts of diarrhea followed by a fever. She'd thrown up in bed. Her father had ground beefsteak leaves with garlic, mixed them with rice liquor, and made her drink it. The fever didn't come down, the diarrhea didn't stop.

I looked at her tongue. Blackened. I took off her shawl and dabbed her perspiring forehead.

"It's some fish I ate three days ago," she said in a thin voice. "Daddy caught them. I said they were probably polluted by chemicals from the shrimp farms."

"Your dad won't be back until late today," I said, looking down at her blistered lips. "You need to go to the hospital."

"Am I going to die?"

"No, silly."

Her teeth chattered. "I'm cold, chú."

I stood up. "Okay, I'll be back shortly."

* * *

The doctor at the town hospital diagnosed typhoid and treated her with antibiotics. He injected syringe after syringe of sodium solution. I came back the next day while she convalesced. She looked even thinner. I held her hand. I knew how close to death she had been.

"I brought you soymilk," I said.

I removed the brown bag and gave her a glass jar of fresh soymilk. She palmed it, her cheeks flushed from the heat inside the small room. "Can I drink it, chú?" she said, and wet her dry lips.

"Sure. It's good for you."

She sat up. I handed her a glass and watched her drain it down, not wasting a drop. Still holding the empty glass in her hand, she looked at me, then at the unlit cigarette between my fingers. "Why don't you light it, chú?"

"I'd rather not," I said and put it back in my shirt pocket. "The smoke will make you cough."

"Am I going home today?"

Home. Her father was like a ghost coming and going in their house. Before I could answer, someone paused at the door momentarily, then came into the room. I shook hands with the doctor and said I was grateful. The doctor glanced at the chart hung on the bedpost and said the girl was improving enough to leave the hospital the next day. I thanked him and he left. She said her stomach still hurt as she turned on her side to put the glass back on the table, and the burn scar on her cheek, salmon-colored, shone in the table lamplight.

"You never told me about your scar. Did you burn yourself?" I asked, pointing at my own cheek.

She squinted at me. I leaned back in the chair under her gaze and shrugged.

"I didn't burn myself," she said finally. "Mom did."

"By accident?"

"She didn't like the fish soup I cooked, said 'Why don't you and your father eat this?' and she threw the bowl in my face."

"Hell," I said, shaking my head.

"Chú," she said, leaning forward to hand me the jar, "don't you want a sip of soymilk?"

"I'm not thirsty. It's for you."

She sat back. "Who brought you cigarettes now?"

"I did. I went to town."

"I'll be back to work tomorrow."

"Take another day's rest. You said your tummy still hurts."

"It's tolerable now, not like a couple of days ago. It hurt bad then and I had tears in my eyes." She was stopped by a sudden cough. "But I'm feeling much better now. I want to go home and check on Daddy. Does he know where I am, chú?"

"Certainly. Did he drop by while I wasn't here?"

"I don't know. He might have done. Before sunrise. He goes to sea very early. I must have been sleeping when he came."

I looked away, hearing her wishful voice. Then she said, "I could've died, the doctor told me."

"Well." I tried to smile. "You're a good girl. You can't die."

"I almost died last summer."

"How?"

"I got bitten by a rabid dog one night when I left Auntie's house. Auntie came to visit me. She sat by my cot, holding my hand. I asked Auntie, 'Would they have to chain me down?' and Auntie said, 'The Buddha will save you. Be good, and nothing will harm you.' This hospital didn't have vaccine. Said it was on back order. Daddy took me back. At dawn Daddy took me on a bus to Huế. I was feverish. The city doctor vaccinated me. We arrived at our hamlet at dusk. Someone was waiting at the bus stop. It wasn't Mom. It was Auntie."

fourteen

Cam said, "Auntie shouldn't come to visit me because she can't find her way around anymore."

That day I took the girl home from the hospital. I went back out on the main road. In the August heat I stopped often because my sandals kept getting stuck in the blistering blacktop. The heat stirred like a white sheet of gauze, hazy and yellow with dust. As a habit, I closed my eyes and then opened them with my head bowed. That way I would not feel dizzy in the blinding glare of the sun. Yet my skin felt tingly under my shirt, and my underarms felt damp. I nodded at a priest who wore a *salako* and held a large white umbrella over his head. He nodded back and walked on with his helper, a local boy, trailing behind, cradling a cloth bundle in his arm. Someone was playing music. Across the street a blind old man squatted in front of a hut, plucking a monochord. Next to him sat a little boy tapping a drum. I dropped three coins in a tin can placed between the man and the boy. The clinking of the coins was lost in the sound of the instruments. I was surprised at the unusual quiet on this side of the street where feet scurried about at high noon and the sun glared on conical hats bobbing up and down the narrow sidewalk.

In the distance, past the white church by the roadside, with its red-tiled steeple topped by a wooden cross, I saw Miss Phượng. She looked as though she was waiting for a bus, except there was nothing around but a barren plot next to an elementary school. She moved across the lot.

"Auntie," I called out to her.

She shuffled over to a chair inside an empty classroom and sat down. The wall next to the much-faded blackboard displayed an old map of Vietnam. On the chalk rail were wooden compasses, a metal triangle, a square, and a protractor.

"Where were you going, Auntie?" I pulled up a chair and sat next to her.

"I'm on my way to see Cam. She's back from the hospital today, isn't she?"

"Yes, Auntie. She's fine now. And why are you in

here?"

"The heat out there really took my mind away."

"How's that, Auntie?"

"It seemed to blank my mind for a moment. I didn't know where I was."

"Do you know where you are now, Auntie?"

"In a while."

"Do you remember how to get to her place, Auntie?"

She nodded. "Where am I?" she said.

* * *

Yet, she could remember what her father once told her the day the last emperor had decreed the abrogation of the concubine system, which set free all concubines from the court, leaving each the right either to return to her family or to stay on to tend the previous emperor's necropolis.

That night her father wished Ân-Phi a good night's sleep and left to return to his quarters. Far in the corners of the garden foxfire glowed on deadwood, and the sound of the piano trickled in the stillness that smelled like rain. He stopped at a magnolia tree where Ân-Phi had hung a pot of dawn orchids on a branch. Moss burned a phosphorescent blue on the tree trunk, and the magnolia blossoms became so thick in his throat that he had to close his eyes. The tree was only her height the day she was inducted into the imperial palace. Now it stood like a giant umbrella. She was going home. What would become of her?

The sound of the piano drifted from her chamber, a melody he had never heard before. Listening, he marveled at the touch of her fingers, at the Heavens' whim to have robbed her all of her faculties but her flair for the music. Every note clear, strung together like a garland of sorrow tossed out into the blackness of the night.

* * *

Six years after Ân-Phi left the imperial palace, the last emperor of the Nguyên dynasty abolished the age-old eunuch system. Her father became a civilian, after sixty-three years of dutifully serving the royal families.

With the money he saved, he built a house in the hamlet of Upper Đinh-Xuân, fifteen kilometers southwest of Huế. He was seventy-three years old when he settled in Upper Đinh-Xuân. Occasionally he visited his former fellows. One eunuch married a lady-in-waiting, and their wedding became the village joke. His deputy, upon leaving the palace, married another eunuch. Her father presided over their ceremony, blessed them, and wished them many happy years together. He understood the urge to have a companion, man or woman. Yet some like him chose loneliness rather than the persistent throb of longing.

Three months after he settled in Upper Đinh-Xuân, he came face-to-face with an aching void in him that had refused to fill. He missed his many years with Ân-Phi.

* * *

Bộ did not have to wait long at Sir Đông Các's residence. Ân-Phi's father was in his early sixties, the only one left of the four supreme mandarins of the court – the French had ousted the rest. The house was warm. A brazier crackled under the mahogany divan. Bộ admired the ironwood pillars and crossbeams held together by mortise and tenon that gleamed, dustless.

Bộ immediately inquired about Ân-Phi. An uneasy silence fell.

"My daughter no longer lives here with our family," Đông Các said.

"Where does she live now, Sir?"

"Let me consult with my wife. Please wait."

Bộ drew a deep breath and leaned back in his chair. Đông Các returned. A corner of his mouth jerked as he said, "My daughter stays at the Thiên Lăng mausoleum."

The deceased emperor's concubines and some eunuchs had tended the sixty-year-old mausoleum of Emperor Tự Đức, nested among pine hills south of the capital, for many years. Originally there were one hundred and three concubines, most of them long dead.

Bộ's voice dropped. "May I ask why she stays there?"

"She was pregnant."

"Sir? How?" Bộ's voice suddenly rose. "Forgive me."

The corner of Đông Các's mouth twitched again. "It's a mystery to us."

* * *

Bộ arrived at Thiên Lăng at noon. He got off the ferry under the shade of a banyan tree. Distracted, he tripped over a huge serpentine root and lost his shoe. Who had Ân-Phi let into her life? He trod across the Congregation Court between rows of stone elephants, horses, and life-size military and civil Mandarins.

As he emerged from the Worship Hall, he shaded his eyes against the sun. A row of wooden shacks stood in the rear. By an earthen vat an old concubine squatted, washing clothes. She beat and wrung a garment on a gray flagstone. He cleared his throat. The old concubine blinked her rheumy eyes and flashed a toothless smile.

"Aren't you the grand eunuch? You came here some years ago."

"Yes, Madam." He remembered her too. She must have been in her nineties, having tended her emperor's tomb for seventy-five years. He stooped and raised his voice slightly so she could hear. "I was told that Ân-Phi stays here."

The concubine hung her head. Bộ thought she hadn't heard him, but then she nodded.

"May I see her?"

The concubine rose with difficulty. "What is the purpose of your visit?"

"I used to serve her, Madam. I came because I'm concerned about her welfare."

"That she's expecting a baby?"

"Yes." Bộ dabbed at his brow.

The concubine asked him to wait and went into the last shack on the row. When she returned, she brought a eunuch with her.

"Bộ," the eunuch said, "it's a surprise to see you here." He beckoned for the older man to follow him to the last shack and ducked his head to enter. There was a bamboo cot in a corner with white mosquito netting around it. An old woman sat on a low stool by the cot, hunched over a pot of boiling water. She was the midwife. The old concubine shuffled to the cot and whispered into the mosquito net. Bộ heard a voice from inside and the concubine shuffled to the door, waving for the eunuchs to approach the cot. Then Bộ heard Ân-Phi's voice clearly.

"Bộ!"

He came closer and she asked him to roll up the mosquito net. In the dim light, her face looked pale. Her hair was knotted above her nape and she lay under a woolen blanket, her belly huge. She hadn't aged — she was as graceful as he remembered.

"Ân-Phi," Bộ said, bowing, "it's such a joy to see you again."

Ân-Phi gestured for him to sit, so he lowered himself onto the stool, which was too small for him. The skin under her eyes was moist. "Tell me what you have done since I left."

Bộ told her, eyes half downcast, and she nodded. "How are you, Ân-Phi?" He paused. "I mean in your mind. You were unwell at the end. I always worried about you after you left, wondered … if you were quite yourself."

"I don't remember much of those final months. But I remember you, Bộ. How could I ever forget you?"

He leaned toward her.

"And I know who I am now," Ân-Phi said.

He wasn't convinced. "Who are you, Ân-Phi?"

"I was the second-ranking concubine until our emperor abolished the concubine system."

Bộ peered up at her. "Who served you then, Ân-Phi?"

"You. Then Canh. I was so sad when he died." She paused. "Then I felt as if he were with me somehow. Everything was foggy to me. Later I found letters I wrote with my own hand, but they were from him. They said he wanted me to know he wished for nothing other than to be with me and for me to be happy."

"Did you know he possessed you, Ân-Phi?"

"I never knew anything for certain, Bộ."

Bộ clasped his hands on his knees, thought for a moment, and cleared his throat. "Ân-Phi, do you recall how much Canh adored you?"

Ân-Phi's eyes narrowed in reflection. Her serenity made Bộ's heart well with affection. How many years of her youth had been wasted?

With a sigh Ân-Phi said, "I was sad when he died." She paused. "I've thought of you and him lately. I dreamed last night that you would visit today."

"What else do you remember, Ân-Phi? You used to have a talking myna."

"He died, Bộ." She tried to push herself up and coughed into her cupped hand. "But before he died, he never left my side. I believe Canh was with the bird. In the bird, maybe. Please, pardon my irrationality."

"Do you forgive him, Ân-Phi?"

Ân-Phi gazed at him without speaking. Finally, she said, "Bộ, I'm lucid today, and more so I'm carrying life inside me. Therefore you can see how fortunate I still am compared to Canh."

Bộ glanced at Ân-Phi's belly and for a while neither of them spoke. She told him she would take an herbal medicine to induce labor, because her water had broken. Still numbed by her impending maternity, Bộ asked, "How did your pregnancy come about, Ân-Phi?"

She laced her fingers on her chest. Sadness filled her face.

"Do you know what happened to you, Ân-Phi?"

She nodded.

"Were you clear-minded, Ân-Phi?" He kept his voice even.

Again she nodded.

"Someone who won your heart, Ân-Phi?"

She shook her head. Bộ didn't dare ask anything further.

"My father sold me to a French general. He drugged me and took me."

Bộ suddenly leaned back, lost his balance on the small chair.

"My father kept his position with the court."

* * *

Ân-Phi took the herbal medicine and soon went into labor. From outside Bộ could hear the midwife coaxing her to push, then her moans, then screams. Bộ felt small. He sat down on his heels. With each of her cries he felt a pain cut deep into his bowels. *Stubborn pain.* He heard the midwife, "This can sap your strength quickly and make all your bones ache." He rose slowly to his feet, thinking of all the suffering it took to create life.

An hour later Ân-Phi delivered twin girls. Then she began to bleed.

Inside the shack three candles burned brightly. A wicker basket sat on the cot beside Ân-Phi. In it were two tiny babies wrapped in blankets. The infants' cries pierced the quiet. The midwife held a white towel, blotched crimson. Ân-Phi lay still, sweat glistening on her brow, her eyes half closed, gazing down on her babies. Her lips bled. She must have bitten down on them, hard.

Bộ bent over the women, his voice shaking. "What can we do to stop the bleeding?"

The midwife folded the towel in half and slipped it under Ân-Phi's blanket. "Give her some spinach."

The old concubine ground spinach in a mortar, added water and made Ân-Phi drink. She sipped, one hand holding the basket in which the infants mewled, stopped, then began again.

"Did you feed them?" Bộ asked.

The midwife said, "They cry, but not because they're hungry."

"Bộ."

At her weak voice, Bộ knelt by the cot.

"Ân-Phi," he said softly.

Ân-Phi opened her eyes. "Bộ," came her whisper, "in my life as a concubine …" She paused, wet her lips. "I counted on you. You served me since I was fifteen, I always turned to you for advice, you had my unspoken trust …"

Bộ bowed in silence. Ân-Phi drew her breath in. "Bộ." She half opened her eyes to look at him. "Can I count on you now?"

"I am at your service, Ân-Phi."

"If I die, will you take care of my daughters?"

The yes was in his heart before his mind could acknowledge it. Ân-Phi stopped talking when the midwife changed the towels and the old concubine dunked two blood-soaked towels in a pail of water. It reddened quickly. Ân-Phi drank another cup of spinach water. Her voice was hoarse.

"I'm grateful to you, Bộ. Can you promise me – " she paused, and Bộ leaned toward her " – that you will never tell my daughters who I am, how they came into the world?"

"Ân-Phi," Bộ said. "They will want to know you."

"Bộ." Ân-Phi tried to focus on him. "I had a pair of ruby phoenixes. The emperor gave them to my father as a gift. And in one of my spells of insanity I gave one ruby to a beggar on the street. I want my daughters to have the one I have left." She stopped, her breathing shallow.

The midwife made her drink another cup of water and her hands shook as she held the cup. The midwife replaced the third towel with a fresh one. A brass pan sat on the fire. The old concubine dropped the blood-sodden towels into the boiling water and stirred them.

Ân-Phi closed her eyes to rest. She felt Bộ waiting beside her cot. Steam warmed the room as the bloody towels were boiled, washed, and wrung. Sometime in the evening the old concubine began to feed the infants. Ân-Phi asked to see them. She blinked through her runny eyes to see the tiny humans stir with busy movements, and when she could not see them anymore without straining her eyes, she touched them. Their soft skin warmed her heart.

The midwife changed towels, then felt Ân-Phi's feet. "Getting cold," she said, and started to rub the insteps. Ân-Phi shivered. She asked to hold her babies. Bộ took another blanket from the midwife and gently covered the babies with it, and then the old concubine gave Ân-Phi a quilted one. He stood by her bed, praying silently. Cradling the babies on her chest, Ân-Phi's teeth chattered even after they covered her with two blankets. The old concubine found a coal brazier, built a fire, and put it under her cot.

The babies cried for a few moments, and then fell asleep on Ân-Phi's chest. The three candles burned down, dripping wax onto the hollow dish. In the quiet the coals popped with a warm glow. Bộ sat on the small chair, keeping vigil.

As he looked on, Ân-Phi left.

fifteen

Miss Phượng wasn't home when I came by at noon. I didn't see Cam either. I went back to the lodging house, picked up my notebook, and made my way down the hill then through the pumpkin patch. Late in August the deep yellow of pumpkins bore a shade of fiery red, the setting-sun red, their tendrils crawling freely between the raised earthen beds, the leaves now tattered having aged with a full season, and among them thin-stemmed flowers in golden yellow completely unfurled at high noon. By dusk, upon coming back, I saw the flowers folded in, died.

There were black-and-white-striped skinks sunning on the ledges of rock, dry now at low tide, their long reptilian bright-blue tails curled into a U. They were dazed in the sun as my shadow suddenly fell upon them. The white-daubed tips of the rocks shimmered in the heat. Below, sheltered by rock cliffs, a pool of seawater quivered when a matchstick-thin fish darted across. The water in the rock-harbored hollows was seaweed green, but once I saw one hollow curtained heavily with rock-wall seaweeds, where the water was red as blood. The helping girl once told me the pool water took on the colors of tiny plants or living things that inhabit it.

The day was humid. As I made my way up the dune toward the spreading shade the filaos cast over the slope, a flock of gray-green fruit doves shot up in the air, darkening a corner of the sky. Along the shore, sand dunes shone with a white glare that hurt my eyes. Swallows darted in and out of distant limestone cliffs, and higher circled a peregrine falcon looking for fruit doves.

I sat down under a filao and read April's letter. I forgot how many times I'd read her letter, but I read it again slowly so it wouldn't end, lying on my back, the slivers of sun in my eyes. I covered them with her handwritten letter. The sea-salt odor was thick in the air, waves boomed against tidal rocks, swishing as they ebbed. In the letter, she asked how people made perfume from wild ginger, for I had told her a local − I didn't want to say a girl, the helping girl − had taken me out to hunt wild ginger, the two of us going deep into the marsh behind the dune, where the soil was damp, the ground cool, searching under shade trees where grass didn't grow until we came upon a patch of heart-shaped leaves like a groundcover. Crouching, we could make out little maroon jug-shaped flowers that seemed to bloom out of the earth. They bore a scent like ginger-root. The girl said, while digging up the roots, they made perfume from the oil found in the root. Later, back in the lodging, I came upon a newspaper article written about wild ginger, which said its root was used for many things, one of which was for irregular menstruation.

In the lull between the booming waves I could hear the sound of filao cones falling, their dry scratching against the needle-carpeted ground like a faint rustle of a rodent's feet. I fell asleep, and when I woke the sun had gone from my eyes. It was past noon, and the wind was blowing misty spray off the waves. Walking back, I felt something was missing.

The dry sand was painfully white. The wind blew hard, the dune crests smoked.

I just knew I had to go back to Miss Phượng's house. There was no one there.

The next day I went back, and found her sitting at the

table, sipping her morning tea. When I asked, I received a vacant look in her eyes, her face placid. The helping girl said, "Chú, Auntie won't remember a thing."

"What thing?" I asked.

"I went with Auntie to the hospital yesterday. They kept her there until late."

"Why did you have to go to hospital?"

"Auntie wandered out on the road the night before. Someone found her by the marsh and took her back."

I felt the urge to sit down. Instead, I looked at the large, lacquered painting of the Imperial Throne Room on the wall. Then I went to the door, looking out past the fenced-in garden.

"What did the doctor say?" I asked without turning my head.

"He said she has amnesia. Hospital wouldn't be able to help."

"He's right. I don't think hospitals can help her either."

"Said they have a place in Huế where they look after people like Auntie."

"Yeah." I turned around and walked to the table. She didn't look at me but at a space behind me where the girl was standing in the shadowed nook slicing a lemon. It would be a hot day. The girl always made a fresh jug of lemonade whenever she came in the morning.

"I wish Auntie could be taken care of in her home," I said. "I wish she wouldn't have to be confined to another place. And I won't be able to help her. I'm leaving soon."

"When, chú?"

"In a couple of days."

There was a silence. I glanced at Miss Phượng as she set her cup down and reached for the teapot. Her cup was still full. "Auntie," I said, putting my hand over hers.

She withdrew her hand and rested it on the table.

I looked back at Miss Phượng. She was looking toward the door. "I wonder what I can do today," she said to no one.

I looked at the girl. She lifted her face but kept her gaze at something over my shoulder.

"Let's do something with Auntie," I said.

She nodded.

"What d'you want to do?" I asked her.

"I don't know, chú, it's your idea."

I pursed my lips. "We can make something. Anything. We haven't done anything together and I'll be gone soon. Well."

"I have something at home." Suddenly she stopped with a shrug.

"What?"

"No." She shook her head emphatically.

There was a pile of old newspapers in a corner, and on top of them was a stack of wicker baskets. In them were balls of yarn. I saw sheets of cardboard set against the wall. "Okay," I said, "we can make something with that cardboard."

"Like what, chú?"

I was thinking of an origami bird and before I told her, she blurted out, "Ah, a treasure box."

"A treasure box?"

"Mom had a wooden box. She kept her jewelry in it."

I nodded, smiling. "Okay, that makes sense. We'll make a treasure box out of cardboard, and we'll decorate it. Auntie can watch. Okay?"

"I want to see how you do it, chú."

I told Miss Phượng what we were going to make. She listened, her gaze empty. Then she smiled and said,

"Treasure? For whom?"

"She wants one." I leaned my head pointing toward the helping girl. "Auntie, would you like to see how we do this – together?"

She nodded. "I want to get out of the house too."

I glanced quickly at the girl. She said nothing.

"I don't have glue," I said to her. "Do we have any glue?"

The girl shook her head.

I thought of going into town as I looked out toward the filao standing along the fence. "We can make glue," I said. "Get two cups and I'll show you out front."

She took Miss Phượng by the hand and we went out in the bright sunlight. Cam said excitedly, "How do you make glue, chú?"

"You will see."

"Are you going to do some trick?"

"Purely scientific."

At a filao tree, its trunk straight and hard in smooth furrowed bark, dark red-brown scaled with light gray, I pulled out my pocketknife. They watched as I cut a horizontal curved slit and then notched a deep V above it. I took a cup from the girl and fit the cup's lip into the slit as the sap began to seep down the notch. Miss Phượng's eyes were fixed on the cup, her hands clasped on her abdomen. I let the girl hold one cup and took the other cup. I cut through the bark. A red squirrel darted along the ground, holding a filao cone in its mouth.

Miss Phượng pointed at the squirrel. "What's he doing with the cone?"

"Auntie, he'll store it somewhere and eat it in the rainy season."

"Where?"

"In some hollow tree stump. Or a log. He'll pile the cones around it and cover them with leaves."

Two more squirrels chased each other down the trunk of a filao. They stopped on a cone-laden bough flecked with red awl-shaped flowers. By then the amber sap had just covered the bottoms of the cups. I turned to them. "Smell it," I said, raising the cup to Miss Phượng's nose.

She sniffed it.

"We're going to heat it," I told her.

We brought the cups inside, poured the resin into a pan and heated it. The sharp odor from bubbling resin made Miss Phượng sneeze. While the resin was cooling, the girl and I sat down on the kitchen floor and Miss Phượng sat on a chair, her elbows on her knees, her hands cupping her chin, watching us. I asked the girl how big she wanted the box to be. She thought for a moment, then reached out for the pen in my shirt pocket. Her lips crimped; she began sketching on the cardboard. I watched, surprised at her accurate strokes, clean and straight without a ruler. Miss Phượng pulled her chair up until her knee brushed my shoulder. After a while the girl finished sketching and capped the pen.

"You draw like a draftswoman," I said.

"I can see things, chú."

I took out my pocketknife and cut the cardboard along the outline. I smoothed the rough edges with my hands. "Glue time," I said.

The girl jumped up and brought the pan from the stove.

I glanced up at Miss Phượng. She still looked down at the cutout. "What are you making?"

"Auntie," I repeated, "a treasure box."

She sat down beside me, watching me glue the flaps

one at a time, giving time for the glue to dry. The girl helped. My forehead bumped against hers. She laughed a rare laugh and said the smell of resin seemed to come from my hair.

"Do we have anything like gold paint or glitter?" I asked the girl.

She went into the back room where rice grains were stored along with spare furniture and household supplies. She came back with a paper bag from which she took out a small can. I opened it. Gold paint.

"What?" I said, shaking my head.

"I did some drawings," the girl said. "Auntie said they'd look nicer with gold paint."

She shook the bag, rattling things inside it. "Here are the beads, chú."

I started brushing the box with gold paint while she dabbed the corners with glue, then fastened the beads in a geometric pattern she wanted. We worked on it until the sun was high.

When I rose to my feet, holding the treasure box in my hands, Miss Phượng gazed up at me. The girl cleaned things up. I placed the box in Miss Phượng's hands. A smile came on her face. Watching her I felt as if I had been here before and now I was just reliving the moment.

The house was quiet. For a long time after we put away the treasure box, the resin glue still smelled of filao.

* * *

After dinner the girl brought Miss Phượng tea and served me a cup of coffee. Evening came like a stranger cloaked in black outside the window. Fireflies around a row of potted geraniums on the ledge winked like specters.

"*Voulez-vous de la crème avec votre café?*" Miss Phượng said to me.

I stared at her. Then I said in Vietnamese, "I take it black, thank you, Auntie."

I sipped coffee. *What would become of her?*

"Chú." I heard the girl as I was gazing at the blinking fireflies. She asked if I wanted a fresh cup. I shook my head.

After the girl cleaned up and said good-night, I saw that Miss Phượng went to bed, and I went into the guest room. I told the girl someone must be with Auntie all the time, and asked her to stay the night with Auntie, every night, after I left. The girl said she would try after asking her daddy.

I turned on the table lamp and sat down on the chair. On the wall above the table was a Christmas card the girl had drawn. Yellowed along the edges, the card showed two snow figures wearing black top hats and holding hands at the foot of a hill, one taller than the other. Green pines dotted with white flakes covered the hillside. Children in bright-colored scarves and mittens sledded down the hill. She shaded the background pale blue. I looked with much curiosity. Either she copied the scene from a book or imagined it wholly of a snow country she had never seen nor been to. The scene framed the greeting:

Dear Auntie
You are a great aunt
Merry Christmas!

Other than the card, the walls were bare. The table too was bare except for a rectangular tin box in one corner. It could have been a box of chocolates stripped of its wrapping. I opened it. Inside were stamps of different shapes and sizes arranged neatly in layers. Some stamps had come a long way. I looked up at the Christmas card, at her handwriting, neat and clean.

The bed was cold when I slipped in; the pillowcase smelled fresh.

Now the wind blew the filao cones off the trees and the cones fell rolling down the roof. I listened to the wind and closed my eyes, trying not to think. The girl too had slept in this bed. *What did you dream in this bed?*

A while later the wind stopped. I got up, went to the window and sat looking out between the parted curtains. The neighborhood dirt path was dark. I lit a cigarette. A dry bark came. Beyond the window in the garden stood a long-bodied, bushy-tailed creature. No dog had that slender body or pointed muzzle. A fox. As I watched the fox, it dawned on me that it must have seen the cigarette light. Maybe animals also gravitated to light. The fox too, a solitary hunter.

I closed my eyes, holding Miss Phượng's face in them.

sixteen

"Auntie, look here."

I gave her a grass ball I had picked up from a hollow in the sand. She weighed it in her hand, a tennis ball made of sticks and grass and seaweed. "Who made this?" she asked. I shook my head. "I don't know where they came from." The helping girl, tightening her headscarf against the wind, chimed in. "I've seen them before, chú. Daddy said the waves roll them together and the wind blows them up the shore."

I knelt beside Miss Phượng by a clump of grass. The wind blew up the beach and you could hear the sibilance of sand. She watched the grass blades bend and dip, drawing their tips in the sand. Arcs and circles. She said arcs foretold stormy weather, and circles fair weather. She said she hadn't been to the beach in a long time. She asked what lay in a depression between the dunes. The girl said vines, sometimes cranberry sometimes bayberry. Densely clad, they carpeted the hollows in shining green.

We came upon tracks in the wet sand. The girl said, "That fox was out here early." I said, "It could be a dog's footprints." The girl shook her head. "I know they are his tracks." She said his footprints were clean-looking, each with a two-toed, two-clawed impression in front. She stood back and gazed at the tracks where the fox's footmarks suddenly became erratic, gapped. "What is it?" I asked. She squinted her eyes, thought, and said, "Something must have scared him, and I wonder what that might be."

On the wet sand there were shore birds' footprints. As the girl stood back with Miss Phượng watching the sun set, I followed the birds' tracks down the beach until I saw ahead of me a flock of sandpipers, tan-colored, white-breasted, running with the waves. Twilight now. They were still hunting for food, probing every spot of sand, every ripple mark for mollusks. When they saw me, they scooted up the beach in ghostly silhouettes. I followed their tracks until they were washed over by the waves. Alone on the sand stood a solitary sandpiper in a pool of water. The sunset sent red glimmers in the pool. The bird looked out over the sea and gave a lonely cry.

* * *

Before I left, the girl said, "Chú, wait." She ran into the guest room where she would stay for the night with Auntie, and when she came back out she gave me something wrapped in an old newspaper. I unwrapped it. A necklace made of bull nuts. Those glossy black bull nuts she picked from the pond. I felt them. Each of them looked like a goat-horned devil.

"For your girlfriend," she said, biting her fingernail.

"Thank you, Cam."

She shook her head as if in denial of hearing her name.

I wanted to hug her, but she stepped back and ran into the guest room. I called out to her. As she closed the door I could hear her voice, "I hate you, chú."

I hugged Miss Phượng. She held my hands in hers, said, "I don't pay much attention to things around me, and they pass me by. But they come back to me – at least today. Thanks to you."

I walked with her to the veranda. Then she stood back and watched me leave. When I looked back, the door was closed and the windows were lit, and a blurred shadow moved behind the curtains. I stood until the light in the windows went out. Then I turned and walked away.

A Yellow Rose for the Sinner

The smell of camphor when I opened the clothes drawers made me stop. Uncle Vinh had left the white mothballs behind. They had shrunk as small as marbles. The scent was part of my childhood, and I have never forgotten it. Mothballs in every clothes drawer. Such was the tradition back home, but old-fashioned here. Uncle had only two drawers for himself in the five-drawer oak dresser. The other three used to store his wife Faye's garments. The odor of camphor hung in the air. The chest, together with the rest of the furniture, would be sold as parts of the house.

I looked around. The clothes closet was empty. Above the headboard of their queen-size teak bed hung Uncle's oil-on-canvas portrait. Uncle left it for me. He had been mistaken many times for my father. Even Uncle had told people that I was the son he'd never had. He had been a counselor at the Vietnamese Embassy before the demise of South Vietnam in 1975. Right after that, his American connection got him into the State Department. Faye, ten years his junior, was an immigration attorney at her father's law firm in Washington's Chinatown.

I listened to the emptiness of the house. All that was left to tie me to it were my two boxes.

This morning Faye had dropped by early. She had gathered all her personal belongings, then helped me pack up and empty the trash. By five in the afternoon, we were done when Mr. Kim—her lover—arrived in a station wagon. I hauled the last suitcase into the wagon's trunk and Mr. Kim snapped the tailgate shut. He looked at his watch. The seven o'clock flight to San Francisco was waiting..

We embraced. Keep in touch, Auntie, I said.

She looked up, swept back her hair and brushed it over her ears, past her tear-shaped earrings of sparkling amethyst. I hope to hear from you again, Minh. And …

Say it.

Just think about our old days when you look at the photograph I gave you.

I remembered her framed photograph of an anonymous street corner in the snow.

She lifted her eyes to me. Her hair slipped down, hugging her face the way I wished I could with my cupped hands: black hair, scissored sharp and even at the jawline, glossy, like a raven's plumage. Any regrets?

I tried to grin but all I could do was make a dent at the corner of my mouth, and my arms seemed long and awkward. She closed her eyes, her lashes glistening. Then she broke away and walked to the car.

Through the window I saw her upturned face overlaid by a blue sky and the maples. For an instant, she smiled.

* * *

I remembered the wedding picture Uncle sent home when I was in high school. The bride in the wedding portrait shone with a such ravishing elegance that I fell in love with her. Uncle was my mother's only brother. Uncle brought me out of Vietnam in 1976, one year after the Communist takeover, and paid for my college education and graduate work. I was twenty-four with a master's degree in political science from St. Joseph's College in Illinois.

On Valentine's Day Uncle wore his favorite jacket, which he saved for special occasions. Its banana-yellow fabric shimmered in the light of the aquarium. He looked at his watch: six p.m. At any moment the phone would ring. It would be Faye calling from the airport. She had flown to Bangkok with Mr. Kim, her client, two days before to pick up the Vietnamese child that Kim adopted – the case had been handled by her law firm. It was important enough that it had required her presence overseas with her client.

Before Uncle had known of her travel plans, she said to him casually, Kim and I will travel to Bangkok tomorrow for an adoption case. He'll be a father when we return.

When did he call your firm about this case?

Last month, after the New Year.

Adoption? That's news. Why didn't you tell me before?

If it were a child we adopted, I would.

Her face looked stolid.

Now, Uncle reached for the turntable next to the aquarium. Mozart's fortieth symphony rolled in like tiny waves.

Faye would be back this evening. For Valentine's Day. He didn't want to miss their traditional dinner at his favorite French restaurant. He wanted to tell her the long-awaited news about his nomination for the director's job.

He looked up as I came down the stairs. A bouquet of long-stemmed red roses lay on the cocktail table. He saw me gaze at the roses and said, What's wrong?

Why is it always red roses? Yellow is beautiful too.

Red rose means love. You know what yellow rose means? Infidelity.

Uncle. I sat down by him. You're all dressed up. Are you waiting for Auntie?

I am. It's Valentine's Day. Uncle slapped his thigh. I've wasted my time. Let's do something. If you feel like Vietnamese, we'll eat Vietnamese food.

What if Auntie comes back while we're gone?

She won't.

* * *

It was late that night when Uncle woke. He could smell brandy, sweet and wet in his nostrils. He had passed out, his attaché still open, sitting on the cocktail table beside the bouquet of red roses. Damn. He felt dizzy.

He glanced at his watch. Half past midnight.

Where the hell is she at this hour?

She must be with Kim. His temples ached. He had never questioned her whereabouts until tonight. What had happened to the vulnerability that used to make him shudder like a pale bamboo shoot at a flick of her smile?

He heard the creaking of the entrance door. Faye came in, closing the door behind her.

He sat up, the glass still in his lap. In jeans and a cerise knitted sweater, Faye looked as if she had just gone outside to park her car, though her hair was disheveled.

He rose to his feet.

Don't tell me you came straight from the airport, he said.

I didn't. She glanced at him and dropped the key

chain in her purse.

He blocked her exit from the foyer. Where were you? You're in my way.

Stop acting like you're a guest in this house.

What did you say?

It was my mistake to let you go with Kim to Bangkok. You spoke with him way before you admitted knowing him to me.

You have proof of that? The paleness of her lips made her look ill.

He spun on his heel. From his open attaché he snatched a sheaf of paper.

Check the calls I circled. He stuffed the sheets into her hand. All of them. Aren't they his numbers in New York? Kim's office. Kim's home. You know them by heart, don't you?

He had asked her secretary to fax him copies of Faye's phone bills from the last six months.

How the hell did you get our firm's phone bills? She waved them in his face.

Isn't that beside the point? Didn't you say he contacted your firm after the New Year? And who called him last October? Your dad? C'mon. Cut the crap.

Those calls? her voice shot up. They were about the adoption case for this Vietnamese child we've just brought back with us. You feel left out? Okay. I'll fill you in. Kim had also asked our law firm to handle his divorce case.

Ahh, thank you, Uncle said. Well, first the adoption case, now the divorce case. How apropos. Uncle laughed, feeling hatred surging from deep within. Where's the child now?

With Kim. That's where I was this evening.

In New York?

Here in Washington. He now lives in Adams-Morgan.

To do what? Show him how to change the boy's diapers?

I don't like what I hear, Vinh. Excuse me.

She tried to pass him, only to be pushed back by his hand. Through the softness of her cotton sweater Uncle could feel Faye's shoulder blades. How had she and Kim spent the two nights in Bangkok? He conjured up the images, felt nauseated, and pushed them out of his mind. But they returned. And stayed.

Tell me something, he said. How did you meet him? For the sake of my sanity, I don't want to be kept in the dark. He whispered, Please!

Kim is an old friend –

Old friend. Will you elaborate?

She smiled wanly. We met at the very last New Year's reception hosted by the South Vietnamese Embassy. Before it was shut down by the U.S. in seventy-five.

I'm sure you didn't introduce him to me that night. I was there with you, remember?

Yes, you were.

Let me ask you this. Uncle brought the tumbler to his lips only to see it was empty. It threw off his rhythm. His hand shook. I want to see your hotel bill from Bangkok. That scare you? I know your nature, you reserved one room. My damnation is I didn't know what you were doing behind my back. I do now. If Kim is hungry – or hard up – for a warm body, he's knocking on the wrong door. The woman who lives in this house is married. She's no whore.

Faye lunged at him, snatched the tumbler from his hand, and smashed it on the floor. Drunkard! she screamed. You goddamn drunkard!

She stormed upstairs into the guest room and slammed the door.

* * *

That Sunday Uncle made up with Faye. He took her to his favorite French restaurant.

While the waiter served them dessert, the pianist played *Für Elise*. Velvety chocolate mousse glistened with droplets of condensation. Ginger-almond ice cream dusted with crystallized ginger and crushed pomegranate seeds in gold-rimmed goblets. The mustachioed French waiter uncorked a bottle of Malmsey Madeira, sniffed at the aroma and passed the cork under Uncle's nose. He closed his eyes, inhaled the scent of faintly burnt smoky caramel that wafted up, and his mouth salivated. He nodded in approval.

Faye sipped her wine. Uncle watched the smooth curve of her throat. A black mole dotted her collarbone. She looked ripe in her short, suede jacket the color of pineapple, its front unbuttoned to expose her stretchy gold satin blouse.

I don't know how to put it, Uncle said, but I feel like this is our first anniversary, not eleventh. And you know why?

I won't guess.

You look … voluptuous, like the evening in Nova Scotia.

She wore no makeup beyond a touch of lipstick, yet that touch was lustrous. Her pencil-thin eyebrows were plucked to arch with a drooping curve toward the ends, which gave her face a haughty look. She could scythe you with her eyes.

He met the cautious gleam in her eyes, stopped, and took a sip of wine. Its long silky finish left a smoky taste on his tongue. He had retained this image of her from that first evening of their honeymoon eleven years before. The rest was blocked from his mind. The first time they met, her haughtiness had pierced and deflated his manliness as if she had just slapped him in public. Now, he owned that pride, the arrogance of a domesticated lioness, and it salved his ego. Her proud look was emphasized by the shape of her jaw, now that he noticed – a firm, round jaw. Only when she flicked her face away did he glimpse the fleshiness under her chin.

What's on your mind, Vinh?

Our relationship.

You mean the lack thereof. Faye caressed the shining bowl of her silver spoon.

Uncle rinsed his mouth with a sip of wine. His tongue still tasted the roasted pigeon with wild mushrooms. Just give me a chance to make it work again, that's all I ask.

And if I don't?

She bit down on a pomegranate seed, hard, between her front teeth. The provocative glare in her eyes yanked him forward, his face inches from hers.

Look, his voice suddenly softened, I just want to protect our relationship. He held his breath. And our future.

His eyes drilled into hers, a cat's dilated, empty eyes. The wine made her face flush. She pushed away the chocolate mousse, jerking her face upwards with a sharp intake of breath.

Our future? she said. And what is it based on? Love? Trust? You fill in the blank. I'll be back. Excuse me.

Faye dabbed her lips with the napkin, then rose and

headed toward the ladies' room. Uncle leaned back, watching her. He glimpsed the whiteness of her thighs through the split of her striped mock sarong in silk chiffon wrapped at the waist. He imagined Kim's hand sliding up her thigh through the slit. Suddenly it grabbed him. Did she wear it for Kim tonight? The evening was still young, and how did he know she wouldn't slink out of the house after they got home?

Could a brute like Kim tire of such a voluptuous body?

Uncle let his gaze fall on Faye's unfinished ice cream. It was melting in vanilla-yellow streaks down the side of the bowl. He ate a piece of chocolate mousse. He leaned back, chewing slowly, then looked around the room. The walls were the color of *crème de menthe* with whipped-cream trim. He loved the luxury of enough distance between the tables only this French restaurant could offer.

He felt violated now as he sat alone.

* * *

Late that night when Uncle woke, he hadn't heard Faye come in.

He opened the guest room door—they had slept separately. In the dark he could smell a scent of jasmine. A white flash lit the room. A thunderclap cracked. He glimpsed the bed, and in silence took a step toward it, using his hand to trace its edges. The room slowly emerged, and he saw Faye, the quilt peeled back to her abdomen.

Uncle sat down and touched her face. Her hand clasped his. Her palm was soft and warm. He lowered his face, sought her lips. They opened, timid, then yielded to the moistness of his tongue. Her eyes flew open. She jerked her face away.

What on earth … She gasped, raised herself up on her elbows. Vinh, what are you doing in my bed?

I'm still your husband.

He braced himself over her, staring down into her eyes. She pushed him away and sat up. He banged her down against the pillow. Her hair bounced. He heard her yelp.

He flicked on the light on the night table. Been there all night with him again, haven't you? Uncle said.

So? She stared back. That's my business. Get used to it.

He could have been calm, but what he saw on Faye's bosom caused him to explode. What is this?

Scratches like a cat's claws.

Faye squirmed under the white satin quilt. She moved her bare arm across her chest to cover herself.

He did this to you? Vinh said. Sadist! And what's this smell? You never wore this perfume before.

Everything in him suddenly collapsed. Why did the sight of the scratches on her breasts strike him? Jealousy? Loneliness? He couldn't fake it any longer.

Bring the light closer!

Faye thrashed her head on the pillow. Interrogate me, you brute –

Uncle backhanded her. He bent down, baring his teeth in her face. You like this? He mashed his fingers on her chest as if trying to smear the scratches. Or maybe you wanted to please that bastard, eh? Tell me. Did you? Did you? His eyes blurred. You never weep for me, you never scream for me … just because … just because –

He choked, his chest about to burst. He had done

everything to satisfy her fantasies and desires – all but ...

Say it, Vinh, say it. Why? Why did this marriage go to hell. For eleven years – don't tell me I didn't try. Say it. Or I'll say it for you.

She was kneeling on the bed. Before he could grab her she jumped and ran into the bathroom. The door banged shut. Furious, he twisted the doorknob. He pounded on the door.

Stop it! Christ, stop it! Faye said.

He heard her as if from deep in a barrel. The madness drummed in his ears. It was the sound of his fists banging on the door. I rushed out from my bedroom.

Uncle! I grabbed his shoulder. C'mon, Uncle. Please!

Uncle hit the door with his shoulder. The door frame shook.

I'm not finished with you, he said. Don't you run away. Open up. Goddammit, open up!

Inside, Faye shrieked. You bastard! You don't own me. You don't own my body. You might own the marriage paper, but I don't want that. Stop banging. For God's sake, just stop!

The door gave. Faye stood barefoot on the mosaic tile, holding a razor blade to her throat.

Uncle stopped.

No! I shouted. Oh, no. Don't!

You take one more step, Vinh. I'll kill myself.

Alright. Uncle pointed his finger at her. You know where you stand in this house now. I want you to remember – He turned to me. Don't you try to corrupt him. He's innocent – the only one not yet corrupted in this house.

* * *

By the time I got back to the house, the streetlights were on. Faye was toting a suitcase down the stairs.

She wore a short-sleeve teal T-shirt, stretch lace, tucked into a white linen skirt. Under the scalloped lace I could make out the shape of her braless breasts.

Where have you been? Her forehead glistened with perspiration.

You look like you've just come in from this heat.

No, I've been packing.

Oh. Going somewhere?

San Francisco.

Business trip?

You could say that. She knelt by the suitcase and threw its lid open. Looking to open a law office in Frisco myself.

What? You not coming back?

For a while.

I'm moving out, too. Tomorrow.

Where? She stood up straight, eyed me.

In this area. On Reservoir Road.

Well, well. She sat down, arms crossed over her knees. That's news. Why didn't I know that?

Because I made up my mind this morning.

On the oriental rug, next to the suitcase, sat a leather club bag, its exterior pockets unzipped. A garment bag lay on the sofa and an expensive-looking leather attaché in glossy black was on the cocktail table.

You need help with these? I asked.

Well … She tried to close the suitcase.

I helped her pat down the garments, and then she put her whole weight on its lid while I zipped it up. I could smell her perfume as she glanced up to thank me. She had bags under her eyes, dark and puffy.

Auntie, what happened to your eyes?

I haven't slept much the last two nights. She blinked as she looked away.

I stood up and tapped the suitcase. Where do you want it?

Can you leave it in the foyer? I'll have the cab driver carry it out tomorrow.

Sighing, I lugged it to the foyer. You're going to carry all these yourself in Frisco?

A friend of mine will be there to pick me up. Don't worry.

She rummaged through the club bag, her slanted shadow behind her on the oriental rug. In the stillness I heard the humming of the air conditioner. *Why is the house so quiet?*

Where's Uncle?

Haven't seen him. She started zipping up the outside pockets on the club bag.

So ... I felt the tightness in my throat. This is how it ends.

Yep.

She picked up the bag and walked to the foyer where she set it beside the suitcase. She was barefoot, her toe-nails gleaming cherry-red, her feet gliding on the oak floor with the agility of a cat.

How long will you be gone?

A few weeks. She unzipped the garment bag on the sofa to look over her suit. By the way, I called you earlier today – before noon.

I was over at the front office, I said. Uncle got the promotion.

Is that so? Faye said, eyes dilated. Don't you love politics?

I sat down in the armchair. Anything important that

you called about?

No. She fastened the garment bag and then ran her hand down its length to smooth it. I just wanted to get out of the house for a while. I've been cooped up here all day and it's starting to get to me.

We still can go somewhere if you want. Where would you like to go?

A movie, a bar. She shrugged. A walk to the waterfront. I don't care.

I didn't know you liked taking a walk.

I don't. She chuckled while clicking open the attaché. She knelt against it, the table's edge cutting into her abdomen, and I caught myself looking at where her lace shirt stretched taut.

Let's have dinner together, I said.

We can take my car.

* * *

We got back at eleven. Faye pulled up at the curb, letting the car idle.

Should I go back in? she said, gazing at the house.

Still our house, I said.

Till tomorrow. A smile barely flicked at the corner of her mouth.

It's late. What time do you leave tomorrow?

Now, Minh, don't worry about my bedtime. She patted me on the back of my hand. But I'll leave at four in the morning.

I'm just worried for you.

Okay. Then join me for a brandy.

She found a spot up the street and eased her Volvo in, and we walked back. I watched our shadows on the sidewalk. Tomorrow she would be in San Francisco, and me somewhere else but here. For the first time I felt drawn to her as a friend.

We sat down on the bean bag in the living room. Outside the window the sky was opaque like the milk froth on a cup of cappuccino. Then suddenly the room lit up as the full moon peeked out of the clouds.

How did you find out about that place? Faye asked about the restaurant we had dined in.

It's Lan's favorite restaurant.

Ah, your mysterious sweetheart. The moon lit up half of her face tilted at me. How is she?

We're getting serious. Very serious.

You've never told me about this. I know you're not secretive by nature.

Because you two have been unhappy with each other, I didn't want to sound like a happy idiot.

Faye's eyes gleamed in the moonlit room.

That's marvelous, she said. I wish I could trade eleven years of my life for what you have. She looked up at the moon. I remember when I was a child, I lived up the bank of the Perfume River in Huế. At night the boatmen would play their flutes when they docked their ferries. My childhood fantasy was … She hung her head to one side. An elegant scholar was sitting under a weeping willow. He was playing the flute for me.

I held myself still.

There was this cute little gray squirrel in our backyard this morning, Faye said. He came out from behind the maple and hopped on the bench. He sat there and watched me. I wanted to reach out and stroke him, but I was afraid he might run away. She swallowed. You wondered why my marriage went to hell, and why our family problems finally put us at the crossroads. Call it soap opera, but I wedded Vinh eleven years ago only to remain a virgin because of his impotence. Yes: I remained a virgin until I met someone at a New Year's party at the Vietnamese Embassy in 1974. I became pregnant and had an abortion. She sucked in her breath, her chest rising. I believe there's a void in each of us that that can never be filled. I've tried for years to shovel dirt into that void by throwing myself into my job, and in all-night mah-jongg games, where the day begins at nine in the evening. But I'm not getting any younger. You know what I always wanted? A baby. I crave to suckle that tiny human being in the cradle of my arms and rocking my baby to sleep humming a tune from my childhood still etched in my mind.

I looked at her and finally saw a face without a mask. I had ached for her. But that flame abated whenever I was beside her because of her coldness. Now I felt awkward as I placed my hand on her shoulder and, bending my head, said I was sorry. In silence she swallowed her sobs, then to stop shaking she pressed a palm against her lips and bit hard into its heel. Slowly the shaking passed.

Who was this man you met? I asked.

Kim?

Mr. Kim. I'm sorry, I didn't mean −

I know. I never told you my secret. She dabbed her eyes with her fingertips. I take the blame for letting on.

I was sure what she revealed was only one of many secrets. I had always been an outsider to their world. Yet she must have found something in Mr. Kim besides his virility, perhaps a kinship that stretched beyond love.

He's also my confidant, Faye said. Legally, I'm married to Vinh, and … of course, he can't father a child for me. But I don't want to have a child born out of wedlock with Kim. That's why he adopted a Vietnamese child, in case Vinh refuses to give me a divorce.

She sipped her brandy and raised the tumbler to my lips. I took the tumbler from her hand and swilled it. The cognac burned my throat, stung my nose, and my eyes watered.

Her hands clasped behind her head, she slid down. I rested my head on her stomach, and I could feel her breasts heaving as she breathed. Her breathing came and went like the sound of distant waves.

You ever sleep with her? Her voice sounded husky.

No. I could smell the brandy in my breath. Her perfume got into my lungs, and I felt the back of her hand, as soft as satin, caressing my feverish throat.

Would you sleep with her if you found a chance? Would you? Her throaty voice hovered above me like a long filament of syllables.

Yes.

I thought so.

She combed my hair with her fingers, then, slowly, in a circling motion, her fingertips massaged my scalp. The sharpness of her nails shot a prickling sensation along the back of my neck. Then I felt them behind my ears. I buried my face in her abdomen. Its softness yielded. She sucked in her breath. I found her hand and snuggled its palm against the side of my face. Her fingers crawled down to the corner of my mouth. Her voice dropped to a whisper, You ever wanted me?

Yes.

She took my hand and slid it toward her mouth and bit its knuckles.

Like you want her?

Yes.

She cupped my upturned face. Her nostrils quivered.

A desire suppressed so deep within me broke to the surface when I clung to her like a hungry baby to his mother's breasts.

* * *

It started to rain. The wind picked up, the curtains fluttered. A thunderclap sent vibrations through the walls. I laid my head on her heaving chest. Her heart pulsed to a steady beat. On the charcoal bean bag the white of her body shimmered.

I'd better get going, I said, sitting up.

At this hour?

I'm moving my stuff to my new place. I should be done at first light.

She pulled my face toward her.

I'm sorry, she said. I'll never forget the love you have for both of us. Just don't hate me.

Loud thunder drowned out her words.

The Yin World of Love

It was summer when she arrived in Vietnam from China. Summer was the season of tropical storms and heat. The sea was rough during the whole journey. The warm breeze was dry, the sky blue. The coastline came into view, and then disappeared. Sand-yellow, ocher, then brown. An older woman stayed close to her. The night they approached Hanoi she lay awake. She lost track of time between sleeping and waking. In her sleep, she heard the murmur of the sea, the shrill call of a gull, the sound of waves. Summer blue sky, white lines of distant shores. The sea smelled acrid and warm like unwashed bodies. The sky grayed as rain clouds gathered. Then the sky and the sea became one, so immense she felt as small as a grain of sand. That night, unable to sleep, she put on the shawl her mother had knitted for her. Its wool smelled fresh. She pressed it to her face, inhaling the scent. The older woman asked if she felt sick. She feigned sleep and closed her eyes to hold back her tears. She understood then what it meant to leave her mother for good.

* * *

Eleven was a beautiful age. Carefree and happy just being with her mother. At the riverbank, she watched people washing clothes, beating them on the steps. Women and children picked soapberries along the bank stepped with flagstones. She watched children her age pick out round seeds, brown and shiny, and put them in their pockets. She asked her mother why they collected them. She told her that they pierced the marble-like seeds and strung them together to make necklaces. She watched two boys, perhaps brothers, crushing soapberries and throwing them into the shallow water. Moments later, fish floated up. She came near and saw the fish afloat in the current, their scales gleaming silver. She asked what kind of fish they were.

"Minnow," the older boy said.

"Can we eat them for food?" she asked.

"Don't taste very good. Use them as bait."

"Can I try?" She took a handful of soapberries from the boys, walked to the river's edge and tossed the broken fruit into the water. The boys watched her as she gazed at the river. She felt a surge of excitement, knowing that she must be pretty for them to stare so raptly. The water was frothy, flowing downriver from the landings where women washed clothes. She saw her mother waiting on the bank, her little figure dark in the afternoon sun. She thought the fish must have gone home to sleep since none came for her soapberries. She glanced at the boys standing behind her. "Where did they go? They don't like the fruit any more."

"They don't eat 'em," the older boy said. "The foam kills 'em."

She looked down at the water again. "I don't understand." She decided to walk upriver to her mother. But as soon as she left the boys called out, "Hey, come back. Fish. Fish!"

Fish drifted on the current. All minnows. The older

boy said there must be a school of them moving through. They spotted other fish, green-backed, silvery-sided, among the minnows. "Smelt! Smelt!" the younger boy shouted. She asked if they were good to eat, and the boys, snatching them up, said yes.

"Can I have some?" she held out her hands and they dropped three smelt, wet and shuddering, into her cupped hands. She headed upriver, her back stooped, afraid of dropping the fish, and when she looked back downriver at the two boys, they were bending over the water's edge. The older boy looked up and looked at her. He straightened his back, shading his eyes against the red sunset. When she looked again, he was still watching her with the setting sun in his face.

* * *

From Vietnam, she wrote to her mother every other day, saving sheets of porous paper and giving them to the matriarch at the end of the week to send home. The matriarch loved her penmanship and studied each letter. She told her, "Xiaoli, my handwriting on the best day doesn't come close to your calligraphy. You express your thoughts beautifully."

Their letters took a few months to come and go. She almost cut into the first letter she received from home when she hastily scissored the envelope. A sheet of yellowed paper bore her mother's writing, the ink smeared on each downward-slanted line. The letter had no date. It took a while for her to recognize her mother's voice in the handwriting. Her mother had written the letter over several days and left gaps between her thoughts, always preceded by the line, "I'll come back later."

One night, unable to sleep, her mother sat up and began knitting a white sweater with a lavender hibiscus on the front for her. "It'll look pretty on you, darling. Tonight, when I got up for a bowl of water, I passed your cot and could almost smell the honey locust I used to wash your hair with. Old smells in the house. I use them to tell my way around at night. The one I most want to smell is your skin the nights you slept with me."

The letters from home came once every three months, one sheet each time, different ink colors from letter to letter. "I buy ink pellets only when I need to write you," her mother wrote. "Whatever the store has that day." She saved all the letters her mother wrote. She studied their colors and the tiny, notched edges, imagining their journey from one relay mail post to the next by carts, by runners, traveling on rivers and creeks to Vietnam by basket boats, from town to town until they reached her. If only she could stuff herself into an envelope and go home!

In the early days, the writing paper was so porous and veined with bamboo fibers it pricked her hand. In those days, she would get homesick whenever something familiar would come to her in the day or night. The sound of a woodpecker drilling a tree outside the window made her think of the *ah-oh* of the mourning doves at home; the sound of a woman vendor's voice calling out her breakfast specialty as she ambled through the neighborhood alley brought back the rich egg aroma of pastries her mother made at dawn.

She missed the wall of her school, next to the much faded blackboard, displaying an old map of China. On the chalk rail were wooden compasses, a metal triangle, a square, a protractor. The school was poor, so the students took turns looking for white clay to make chalk for the teachers. On the day her turn came, her mother walked with her to distant tracts of paddies where the soil was gray. They would wrap clay clods in a hemp bag and dissolve them in water at home. When the clay settled, her mother taught her how to roll it into finger-shaped sticks and let them dry, so her teacher could use them as chalk. Sometimes when school supplies became scarce, she went with her mother to the hills to scour bog myrtles to make ink. With a basket hooked on her forearm, she left home with her mother while the morning sun was still mild. She had never seen the bog myrtle fruit until she saw their purple flowers coloring the brow of the hill. She plucked the berries, took them home, and mashed them. She boiled the liquid until it turned dark purple. The homemade ink lasted three days and gave off a strong stench. Some of her classmates' ink lasted much longer because they mixed it with alum, which cost more than rice. So, every three days she would go back to the bog myrtle hills. She resented the bog myrtle ink. Its foul smell made her miserable. Her mother held her against her breast a long time and told her to have faith in Heaven, faith in the order of things to be bestowed on mortals who cared and believed. She kept her mother's words in mind and believed in a faith that could defy even death.

One autumn day, rain fell all morning. Then it rained again into the next day and the next, a damp wind that never seemed to cease. Coming home from school in the afternoon, she saw a village messenger beating a gong as he raced up and down the dirt road. "Each house, each man, five bags of sand," he hollered. Flood again, she thought. But this one could be bad, because the village had already mobilized all the men from fifteen to fifty years of age to guard the dike.

When she got home, her mother was putting on her woven rope raincoat, ready to leave the house. "Where are you going, Mother?"

"To the village cooperative," her mother said. "Come with me. We have to buy sand and jute bags and carry them to the dike tonight."

As she closed the door, a black spider fell dangling in the doorway. "Wait here," her mother said, and went back inside. At the ancestral altar, she lit a joss stick and prayed. Xiaoli watched the spider. It stopped descending and seemed to wait for her to go away. She swatted it and it wriggled on the doorstep.

Her mother put on her straw hat and took her by the hand. "Let's go," she said, "before it gets dark."

"Why'd you have to pray?"

"The black spider is a bad omen."

"Of the flood?"

"I prayed for us to be spared."

She helped her mother carry the jute bags and sand home. They made five sandbags and hauled them to the dike in the twilight.

On the dike, villagers were banging pans and gongs and beating drums. Megaphones called people to spots along the dike that needed to be fortified. She clung to her mother's arm as they jostled through the crowd. Papaya torches lit the night and the rain smelled of burnt leaves.

Men and women worked to reinforce the dike. Wives and daughters came to help their husbands, fathers, brothers. The sky was black, the river and the dike lit only by torches. The drums beat steadily. People moved about like ants, dragging sandbags across the rain-slick dike to places that had to be buttressed. After midnight, the river crested. The megaphones blared out orders: "Dike about to break. Run!" Water surged through gaps in the dike, and people splashed through the current toward higher ground. The frantic beat of drums knotted her stomach. Torches were tossed away, sizzling in the floodwater. Ashes floating like fireflies carried the smell of burnt papaya.

Water rose swiftly to their chest. They reached a hillside shrine, but people were already packed inside. They sat on the steps in the downpour, watching people crouched in the darkness under trees. Her mother cradled her, shielding her head from rain.

"Same kind of flood when I just had you," she said, "when you were barely a month old."

She raised her head. "Was Father with you? In the flood?"

"No. He went back to Vietnam."

"Why? What did Father do? You never told me."

"He works for the greater good."

"What does that mean?"

"He works for his country – in a dangerous line of business."

"But if someone kills Father, who will take care of us?"

"You always have me, darling. And I always have you." Her mother smiled at her affectionately. "Now, just rest. It's going to be a long night."

She closed her eyes, imagining a river that was like the rush of water surrounding them. A thunderous noise blasted through the air. Then shouts – "Dike broke!" – followed by cries in the dark. She shut her eyes, imagining a river, this wild river, overflowing her village, drowning livestock and pets. She thought of her house, then dimly of what her mother said about her faceless father before she fell asleep in her arms.

* * *

One day her mother came home late from her tobacco-stripping job in another village. She worked odd jobs. Nothing lasted long. She had calluses on her hands that she could not even pare with a knife. When there was no work, she set up a stand selling ginger sweetdrops in the alley outside their house, or knitted shawls for people until her fingers and hands ached. Xiaoli saw her coming in with glazed eyes. The bog myrtle ink smelled sour, and the brush she wrote with smeared it across the porous paper. The bamboo fibers had ruined it. Tiny splinters from the paper went into the heel of her hand. Her mother examined Xiaoli's hand by the light of the oil lamp. After she pulled the bamboo splinters from her hand, she padded it with a handkerchief. Her face looked grim, her fingertips browned from the tobacco leaves. She said, "Xiaoli, I'm sending you to Vietnam. You'll be indentured to a Vietnamese family to pay off our debt." Shocked, she looked at her mother who took her bleeding hand into her own. "I owe people money." Her mother's shoulders felt soft and bony, and when Xiaoli wept into her chest, she smelled sweat and tobacco.

In bed later that night, Xiaoli listened to the stillness, to the sound of oxcarts creaking along the road, but after a while she heard nothing. The air was hot after three weeks of dry weather. So much water had evaporated from the pond that you could see the mossy bottom. The rush mat was warm, and her mother was still awake, lying on her side. Her hair covered half her face. Her eyes gleamed.

"What keeps you up so late?" her mother said.

"Do you want me to go to Vietnam, Mother?"

Her mother's chest heaved, and she said nothing.

She spoke into her mother's chest. "Will you miss me when I go, Mother?"

"I will," her mother murmured.

"I know deep in your heart you don't want me to go, do you, Mother?"

"My heart will say no, but my head and mouth will say yes."

Her mother stopped speaking.

"Mother?"

"What, dear?"

"Where will you get the money to buy my ticket?"

"You'll be on a boat. I don't have to pay."

She rubbed Xiaoli's back for a while and then picked up a palm-leaf hand fan and fanned her daughter. Slowly Xiaoli felt herself disconnecting from her mother and slipping into a dark vacuum with nothing to grab, nothing to pull herself back with, and in that vacuum she cried out "Mother!" and woke. Her cheek still pressed against her mother's bosom, she felt her mother's warmth and then a stifled sob from deep in her mother's chest.

The Weaver of Điện Biên Phủ

She sat by the window of her hillside stilt house with a puddle of afternoon sunlight in her lap, her hands resting on a spindle across her thighs. The wall clock chimed five times. In another hour, the fog would move in now that it was the month of March, and the warmth of the day and the last glimmer of sun would be gone. She would wake in the early morning and the fog would still hang in the valley, and the cold would leave a film of ice in the basin out back.

In the early years, she sold her tapestries on consignment at the market that convened at dawn along Provincial Road 41 on Sundays. The Thai women came from neighboring hamlets, dressed in black satin skirts, and sold poultry and pigs and sun-dried fish, wild tobacco and cottonseed and sugarcane. Soon, due to demand, she made tapestries on order only.

She paused and wound the twisted yarn onto the spindle. A hissing sound made her look out the window. Down by the creek that flowed around the foot of the hill, a crested argus was beating its wings rapidly. She listened to its hisses as it danced, its tail spread out, and realized it was breeding season. The bird got down from the log and started feeding on the coarsely-toothed leaves of the blue love, which grew on the moist edge of the creek, bursting violet and blue with their spiky-looking flowers.

The creek coursed through a ravine between two hills.

The water ran low before the rainy season in April. In the creek's shallow riffles, water-willow grew in large colonies. The banks were rocky and slippery where, years before, she'd broken her ankle when she came down to fetch water. In their rock-strewn crevices, limestone fern sprung out in masses.

Beyond the rocky bank, the next hill dropped gently to an arc and the sun reddened its dip above the valley floor. She squinted into the glaring hillside as suddenly heard children singing. A giant silhouette, followed by five small ones, descended the hill in single file. The children's singing voices drifted across the air:

Father's presence
Immovable mountain
Mother's love
Vast ocean
A healthy tree
Always lush with leaves
A child's legacy

The giant silhouette stopped upstream at the foot of the hill, and the children broke off running back toward their hamlet. The seven-foot-tall man always attracted the hamlet children when they saw him. *Come look! Mr. Ibou is here!* He would stop and speak to them, the Viet children, the Thai children, in their mother tongues. Yet he spoke French when he conversed with her because he did not trust his Vietnamese – pitiable, he called it – to make intelligent conversation.

It was Wednesday. His son usually arrived around this time, carrying water in two metal pails to fill her earthen vat, always fetching water upstream, as his father told him to, where the water from the creek wasn't yet soiled by the washing of clothes and the scrubbing of cooking utensils by the Thai families who lived on the other hill. Ibou had his son bring her fresh water every week. Ibou must be sixty-five now, five years older than her. His son was only slightly taller than an average Viet or Thai man, but he was as strong as an ox. Coal-black, and muscular. She'd heard that when he was born, people screamed at how the tiny creature wasn't red like a normal baby, but soot-black with dark, frizzy hair. The medical cadre who'd helped birth him said, "He takes on his father's genes and not a tiny trait from his Thai mother. This is normal, I assure you. Nothing evil." They called the baby "Đam," *Black* in Thai. A healthy baby, and an incredibly strong man in his thirties.

Once, two buffaloes locked horns, grinding and ramming into each other. The people from the hamlet thronged around them, yelling and beating drums to break them up, and then they dumped straw on the beasts' heads and burned it. But the buffaloes stayed locked. Đam walked up to them, grabbed their horns, and pushed them apart.

Now she climbed down the wooden ladder outside the house and stood under the shade of the ylang-ylang tree. She could see Ibou crossing the grassland toward her house, the tall red grass blazing in the setting sun, his silhouette bobbing as he moved along the bank of the creek and through a grove of blood banana. The dark red splotches on their fronds looked bloodstained in the brightness. It was so quiet she could hear the creek, and the air was suddenly tinged with the fragrance of custard, heady and cloying. She shivered as she always did in the shade of the tree, inhaling its scent.

The old man finally emerged in her front yard after climbing a flight of stone steps. He carried the pails like tin toys – by the wooden handles – as he headed to the earthen vat, which sat in the shadow under the floor of the stilt house. He paused as he passed her. "*Comment allez vous, madame?*"

"*Ça va bien,*" she said. "*Et ta famille?*"

He set the pails side by side in the sun. "My family is fine. I'm glad you asked because my wife is now a grand-mother, and my son a father."

"I was thinking about Đam when I saw you coming." She looked up at his dark face, glistening with sweat, childlike and wrinkle-free. "When was the baby born?"

"Sometime after midnight last night. My wife and a woman neighbor delivered the baby."

"I cooked something for him. I thought I'd give it to him when he came. Can you take it back to his family?"

Ibou and his wife lived with their son's family.

"Sure, madam. They will love it. My wife says, 'That lady of Điện Biên Phủ can cook Thai dishes so well, I forget she is Viet.'" He bent so he could see her better, without the sun in his eyes. "My wife always says 'the lady of Điện Biên Phủ' when she speaks about you. I told her, 'She has not aged.'" He scratched his stubbly chin. "It's true, madam, you have not."

She tightened her lavender paisley headscarf, which was wrapped around her rolled-up hair. Let loose, it would fall to her waist in a luxuriant black curtain. "*Merci.*" She looked toward the vat under the house and back at the pails. "You don't need to make another trip. We had a good rain last night. It filled the basin in the back." It had rained heavily, for a change. When the rainy season would set in next month, she would not see his son again for some time – until the dry season in October, which would last through March.

Ibou picked up the pails of water. "I'm going to fill the vat and I'll be on my way."

"Please come up to the house. The pot is heavy for me."

"Yes, madam."

After he climbed the ladder, she could see him dip the wooden scoop into the vat and take a healthy swig. He had to kneel almost to the ground just to fill the vat.

She entered the house barefoot, the bamboo slat floor cool from the air rising from the open, uncluttered space beneath the house. She stood for a moment, feeling the coolness on her skin, then went around the loom to the hearth in the corner of the kitchen, near the second window. She liked the house airy and well-lit, so when she weaved during the day, ample sunlight would come in through the two large awning windows, each propped open with a bamboo rod.

She lifted the lid on a tall earthenware pot as Ibou appeared. He ducked as he came through the door. The floor shuddered. His head brushed the traverse rod, and made the metal loops where balls of colored wool dangled clink.

"I've never come into your house," he said, his eyes darting left and right. "It must be thirty-four years now. *Oui, madame?*"

She believed it was. That year, 1960, she'd left Ha Noi and come back to the valley on the sixth anniversary of the victory of Điện Biên Phủ. She wasn't raised here, but she'd come in 1954 to be a tiny, insignificant part of the military campaign against the French Empire during the siege of Điện Biên Phủ. She was twenty years old then, a singer and dancer in an ensemble.

"Had it not been for the excavation in 1960," she said,

smiling, "you and I would've never crossed paths. And I would bite my tongue in two if I said it meant nothing to me to know someone like you, who shed blood on the soil of this valley."

Ibou nodded solemnly, straightening his back. His head hit the rod again, and the metal loops clinked. "I came back here in 1959. It's been my home ever since. But I never thought I would find another soul like me here, who came out of that hell alive." He wiped sweat off his face with the sleeve of his old army shirt, its original olive color now a dull yellow. "When I saw you in that crowd at the excavation, I knew you weren't Thai. But there were no Viets living on the hills at that time, just Thai. I had to ask around."

"I believe I was the first Viet to make my home here." She pursed her lips, remembering. "Some years ago, I heard about a man who claimed that he was a Điện Biên Phủ war veteran. He'd married a Thai girl and lived in the hamlet of Pom Loi."

Pom Loi sat in a cluster of hamlets along the creek that flowed east to west. Westward, it went as far as Provincial Road 41, which was dotted with hamlets, dusted red from the surrounding hills on a windy day. Ibou lived somewhere in those hills.

"So you met your compatriot, madam?"

"Yes. It turned out he'd seen French aircrafts shot down repeatedly over the valley by our antiaircraft artillery. He was only a civilian living in one of those hamlets on the east side of Điện Biên Phủ Valley – there used to be a Việt Minh antiaircraft deployment ground nearby. He looked embarrassed when he told me the truth. When he was drunk, he'd tell hamlet children that he was an antiaircraft gunner and show them a long aircraft wing that now sat on the roof of his house, collecting rain-water. He told them it came from a French airplane he shot down. Sometimes he'd take the children to a plain a kilometer from his home, where he'd show the children several wrist-sized cartridge cases among a handful of hoes. He told them the cases came from the 37 millimeter antiaircraft projectiles, and that the *bộ đội* used the hoes to dig trenches and their deployment shelters."

"I'm thinking of the human remains," she said.

"I know that, madam." Ibou, nodding, dropped his gaze with a sigh.

Between 1959 and 1960, she remembered, local authorities had begun moving people's remains from the valley to the newly built cemeteries, one of them A1 Cemetery at the foot of the old A1 Hill. Most of the graves had no names on the headstones. This all started a few months after she began her new life in the valley. It was a hot, muggy summer day at the digging site where a large crowd of locals gathered, watching the district reconstruction team digging an old trench, thirty meters long, near the western side of A1 Hill. Some time before noon there came yells. A crewman had just shoveled a leg bone out of the dirt. Then more bones. Skeletons whole, skeletons in pieces. A human skull, then another. Within an hour, they'd unearthed thirteen skeletons. One of them was still in a sitting position, clothes tattered and clinging to the bones, a PPSh-41 submachine gun held in its hands, four grenades strapped to a belt, a little jar of Tiger Balm in one shirt pocket, a fountain pen clipped to the other shirt pocket, and a pouch made of parachute cloth. Inside the pouch was a lock of hair.

For days, she thought about that lock of hair. She imagined its owner, a girl perhaps her age, for most who'd joined the military campaign against the French in Điện Biên Phủ were young. A girl still living with a fishhook in her memory, day after day, from waking moments to haunting dreams that had no scents, no colors, only the lingering melancholy of a love story half-real, half remembered.

"I didn't tell you this," she said, lifting her face to Ibou, her hand touching her brow, as if to pinch the fleeting thought. "But I knew who you were when I saw you at the excavation site, way back then."

Ibou drew up his shoulders. "How?"

She left the hearth and went to the wall between the two windows. She pointed at a graphite-on-paper drawing framed in black bamboo. It was just after dawn in that small drawing. Her entertainment team had performed in the heavy fog before the enemy airplanes took flight. The ravine was the stage, and the artillery men of the 45th Artillery Regiment watched, sitting on the hillside. The 105 millimeter battery units had toiled all night, building out their emplacements and shelters, and now sat hugging their knees, rapt, watching the team perform 'The Ballad of Cannon Pulling' accompanied by a solo accordion. The accordion had been a war booty donated to the performers by the commissar of the 351st Heavy Division. It was red, she remembered, and carved with the words Victory of Him Lam Hills, the first French stronghold at Điện Biên Phủ to fall on March 13, 1954. When she stopped singing, she'd bowed to the men on the hillside. Most of them had nodded off; others were dragging on their cigarettes to keep their eyes open. The accordionist had pulled her aside and said, "Let's play something soft. Let's not disturb their sleep."

Now she watched Ibou studying the drawing. She

could see his mouth moving soundlessly. His gaze shifted to one side of the scene, where three French prisoners, escorted by two small *bộ đội*, were also watching the performance. One prisoner was a black figure who stood among them like a tree – so tall and black against a pale, translucent fog.

She expected him to say something. Finally, half turning his face to her, he said, "I see you and me in there. I was thinking how forty years less one month have passed like the blink of an eye."

"You surprise me," she said. "Forty years less one month?"

"Mid-April, 1954. I don't remember the exact day. What I remember is the rain. I still hear its sound – not like when you're inside a house, no, madam. A primitive sound. It made you shake like a leaf, hearing it in the forest."

She looked at the drawing. Just fog. Then, yes, rain would come. Morning, afternoon, night. It came without warning and would fall for days on end. She remembered the black giant who drew everyone's gaze as he was shepherded through the ravine at the end of the performance. "How did you become a prisoner?"

"Our emplacement was overrun."

"You were an artillery man?"

"*Oui, madame.*" His eyes became still, like he'd just recalled something but decided not to speak.

"You were captured on that day?"

"Two weeks before that, on the first day of the Việt Minh's second offensive. March 30. Our side called it the Battle of the Five Hills. Dominique 1 and Dominique 2, and Eliane 1, Eliane 2, Eliane 4. I know your side had different names for them."

She nodded. "Eliane 2 is our A1 Hill. The terrible hill."

"But on that day," Ibou said, glancing at the drawing, "my fellow soldiers and I were taken to the rear, roughly fifteen kilometers away where we could no longer hear the sounds of artillery and fighter-bombers. Don't ask me if I missed them, madam."

She smiled. "The war might not have missed you either."

He leaned on his arm, his fist resting on the wall above the drawing. He bent his head close to it, taking in the details. "Did he miss it? The artist who drew this, I mean. Are you a friend of his, madam?"

She put her hand over her lips. "We were lovers."

"*Ooh-la-la!*" Ibou turned and looked down into her eyes.

She laughed lightly. Her words seemed to echo in her ears. For forty years, they'd been locked inside her.

Ibou trailed his long forefinger across the bottom corner of the drawing, where the artist had signed his name: Lê Giang. "I recognize his name."

"You knew him?"

"If that's his name."

"His alias. We didn't use our real names during the military campaign for different reasons. One of them was identity secrecy."

"I knew him," Ibou said softly. "He gave me a drawing he did – for me."

"How interesting." She inhaled deeply. "What did he draw for you?"

"A charcoal-on-paper sketch. Smaller than this, I believe. He gave it a title too."

"In Vietnamese? Or French?"

"Vietnamese. But he told me what it meant." Ibou frowned, then smiled. "'Portrait of Brother Tak-Mak.'"

She chuckled at his Vietnamese. "So he drew you. But 'Brother Tak-Mak?'"

Ibou laughed. His laugh sounded like a rumble. "That was what they called me after my capture. During the two weeks in the valley, they interrogated me, and I cooperated. I gave them the positions of our artillery emplacements in the valley and the concentrated fire-power of our headquarters. But they already knew all that. What they wanted to know was our mobile artillery. They had no knowledge of it until they launched their first offensive on March 13. We hid those mobile units and only revealed them when the Việt Minh came at us, and we inflicted heavy casualties on their infantry.

"During the interrogation, there was an interpreter. The interrogator asked a lot about the deploying schemes of our ghost artillery, our transit plan for it … where and how. He kept saying *thắc mắc* and the interpreter had a hard time interpreting the words. Once I knew what they meant, I spoke the correct words, and they laughed and started calling me 'brother tak-mak.'"

His excitement made her feel lively. *Forty years less one month.* She smiled at the phrase. "I'd love to see the drawing he did for you."

"I recognized his signed name. All these years, I thought that was his real name."

"His real name? Trần Khang."

Ibou mused, "He told me he was an artist-reporter for the newspaper of the 351st Heavy Division. He looked so young. But what a gifted young man."

"We were the same age. Both of us were twenty at that time."

Ibou looked down to seek her eyes. "Where is he now?"

"He was sent to the South shortly after our victory at Điện Biên Phủ. The North had prepared for the infiltration of the South as soon as Việt Nam was divided into North and South by the Geneva Convention in 1954. I have not heard from him since."

Ibou dropped his voice. "You never married, madam?"

Her lips formed the word *no* as she shook her head. When she caught him gazing at her, he blinked.

"You're very beautiful," he said. "You must have loved him very much. Did he ever draw you, madam?"

"I'd need to ask him that, wouldn't I?"

Her fluty laugh made Ibou nod, then he, too, laughed.

Destination Unknown

At dusk, lights came on in the town the river ran through. The river, now dark, carried with it the lights like starlights, and cajeput flowers that had fallen from the riverbank floated white on the water.

From a ferry peddler he bought sweet rice cooked with mung bean, packed in a banana leaf, and black coffee in a Styrofoam cup. He ate while the riverboat waited for passengers to board. Then he took off the cloth cover of the birdcage, set the cage on his thighs, and began feeding the myna with leftover sweet rice.

"You like sweet rice or you like papaya?" he said, watching the bird peck a yellow bean from his palm.

"Papaya," the bird said, bobbing its head twice. "Yummy yummy."

"What did Ly give you?"

"Papaya." The bird purred deeply.

"Where's Ly?"

The bird looked around, then bobbed its head repeatedly.

"Call Ly," he said. "Call her." He watched the bird as it fluffed its feathers then called out, long, clear, *Ly Ly Ly Ly*. Then it cocked its head and watched him intensely.

The new passengers were coming on board, a woman and a young girl, who sat down on the bench seat across from him. He smiled at them, and the bird bobbed its head and croaked, "Hello guest!"

The girl's face beamed. "A talking bird!" she said.

She bent forward and looked at the bird. It tilted its black-crowned head, studying her. "What's your name?" the bird squawked.

The girl broke out laughing, covering her mouth with her hand. She had an eyetooth that made her smile charming. "He can really talk," she said to him.

"Yeah. He can mimic all kinds of sounds."

Just then another riverboat passed by out in the broad water, its motor chugging steadily. The myna looked around, shifting on its thin legs and making some deep-throated sounds.

"He heard the boat, I think," the girl said.

"Yeah. He can neigh like a horse, meow like a cat." Stroking the bird on its breast with his finger, he said, "What the cat say?"

"Meow," the myna let out a crystal-clear cat's sound.

"Oh my," the girl said.

"What's your name?" he asked her.

"Kim."

He glanced up at the woman who had been watching them. She wore an indigo blue headscarf, sitting with a carry-on bag on her lap. "Where are you folks going?" he asked her.

"The Plain of Reeds."

"Oh. It must be in the flood season now."

"It already was when we left last week. And where are you going?"

"The Plain." He lied.

"Oh really? Visiting?"

"No. I live there." He knew nothing of the Mekong Delta.

"Well, neighbor, you must've been away then. We had

early flood this year. What d'you do there?"

"I have a fishing boat." After lying the second time he looked down at the myna and then at the little girl. "Kim, you want to feed him? Here. Just give him bits of this." He put some sweet rice in the girl's palm. "Let him pick from your hand what he wants to eat, bean or rice. There."

The girl gently touched the bird's head with her finger. The bird pecked a yellow bean from her palm, tossed its head back to down the food, and sang, "Thank you, Ly, thank you."

The girl laughed. "Oh, you're so sweet." Then she looked at him. "Who's Ly?"

"My lover. I mean my girlfriend." He caught the woman smiling as she adjusted her headscarf.

"The same, isn't it?" she said to him.

"What is?"

"Lover and girlfriend."

"You have a lover?" the little girl said, all perked up.

"Yeah. She's his favorite person. He knows her well."

"Where is she?"

He thought for a moment and the woman said, "Your lover." He glanced at the woman and then at the girl. "She's home."

"When are you going to marry her?" the girl said.

"Shhhh," the woman said.

"I'll ask her to marry me when I get home," he said, smiling.

The girl's face beamed. "You should, I think. Will she say yes?"

"Yeah. I know she will." He picked up his cup of coffee and let the myna drink from it. "She's carrying our child."

"You mean she's pregnant?"

"Yeah."

The woman dipped her head toward him. "Are you serious?"

"She told me yesterday."

"Then I think you ought to marry her. Soon."

"That's what I'm planning to do."

The little girl stroked the myna's back as it dipped its beak in the coffee. Then she said, "Is she a nice girl?"

"She's beautiful."

"What does she look like?"

"Well …"

The woman giggled. "Don't mind her."

He shrugged. "First time I saw her, she was coming down the road one night on this beautiful white horse. I could hardly breathe while I stood in front of her. I knew I would never be the same again without knowing her."

"Oh." The little girl's mouth fell open. "I always loved horses. I wish one day I will have a horse of my own."

"They are beautiful. I have a quarter horse myself. She has a stallion. We ride around together sometimes, late in the night."

"Can she still ride?" the girl asked, raising her eyebrows.

"Of course. Why?"

"She's pregnant."

The woman laughed and patted her daughter on the head.

"Sure, she still can ride," he said.

"Can he stay on her horse's head while she rides?" The girl touched the myna's beak with her finger. "I saw mynas standing on buffaloes' backs."

"Yeah. I'll tell her. We'll try that next time we ride

out."

The riverboat sounded its whistle. The girl sat back on the bench seat, looking at him as he put the cloth cover on the cage.

"What are you doing that for?" she asked. "How can he breathe?"

"Just so he keeps quiet and won't bother other people with his talking."

"Can I hold the cage, please?"

"Sure, Kim." He leaned forward and placed the birdcage in her lap. She wrapped her arms around it, her eyes gone soft and dreamy.

It was evening now, and the river was quiet. The water was dark, red as blood where it ran into seaward tributaries. In the cabin, lights had gone out and the passengers were sleeping. The girl slept, her head resting on her mother's shoulder, the birdcage in her lap secured by her arms still wrapped around it. Some time in the night it began to rain as the riverboat passed a town and its lights, beyond the wooded bank, blinked like diamond dust. He woke hearing the sound of rain and, in its empty cadence, thought he heard her voice. He imagined the sea almond trees around the servant quarter standing solemn, dripping rainwater from their leathery leaves, the fruits ripe and red, and if it rained early in the evening the resident bats would not come out. That was where he had stayed and worked for her husband, who was twice her age, sexually impotent, even before he married her. He had been married before: his first wife gave him a child, but she died. The boy was autistic, and always wore a little brass bell on a neck string; if he strayed from the house even after dark, the tinkling of the bell would help find him. After his wife died, and before the man remarried this woman twenty-five years his junior, a sickness had left him confined to a wheelchair, and sexually powerless.

"Recently, my husband has asked me to do something for him. If I do it, it might help save him from dying." She went into a silence that he didn't want to break. Then she said, "He said he wants me to have a child. That his impending misfortune could be avoided if we have a child to raise as his descendant. He said the severity of one's own evil karma might be assuaged by receiving an auspicious birth of a child into one's life."

He'd often thought of the consequence of their act in that room, driven by her own choice to have a child for her husband. The thought of seeing her carry a child had troubled him: how painful it would be should it become a reality. Then one evening after dinner, having gone back to his room, sitting down on the bed, and taking off his shirt for his bath, he heard a knock on the door. He flung the shirt over his shoulder as he opened it. There she was standing on the dark veranda, arms folded on her chest, back turned toward him, gazing at the grove of sea almond trees.

"Hi," he called out to her.

She turned around. "Can I come in?" she whispered, barely loud enough for him to hear.

He stepped back to let her in and closed the door. In the cage hanging from a ceiling hook, the myna croaked, "Hello guest!"

"Hello there," she said, touching the cage as the bird tilted its head to regard her. Then she spoke without looking at him, "He must be speaking very well by now. Am I right?"

"What he likes to do is birdcalls. He's alone by himself most of the time so he picks up anything he hears from outside."

"Poor little thing."

He draped the cage with his shirt and then dragged the only chair he had to the center of the room, under the naked light bulb hanging from the ceiling. She sat down and he stood, hands jammed in his pockets. Slowly, he sat down on the edge of his narrow bed. She was still in her business suit, a single-breasted navy-blue gabardine and cuffed pant legs, and the air had a scent of her perfume, which he remembered well.

"I hope you've been alright," she said, her hands clasped in her lap.

"I have no complaint. How have you been?"

"Okay." She nodded, then brushed back a strand of hair that had slipped down on her forehead. "I found out yesterday that I'm pregnant."

Something very cold went through him, and he shivered in his bare torso. He simply nodded.

"I figured I was at one point," she said, holding in her breath and then slowly exhaling. "But I wasn't positive of it until yesterday when our physician confirmed it."

He wondered if their personal doctor knew, too, of the truth of her pregnancy. He felt overwhelmed. She ran her fingers through her hair. Her jacket sleeves stopped just at the wrists, where they revealed the white cuffs of her shirt. She lowered her gaze at his bare torso and then looked up into his eyes.

"I want to tell you something," she said, "and I want you to be ready for it."

"Tell me."

"You can't stay here any longer."

He slumped and then immediately straightened his

back. "I hear you," he said.

"You rarely ask questions, I notice."

"I don't think my questions would change anything."

"You don't even want to know the reason, do you?"

He fixed his gaze on her face. The hollow in him was so deep he saw her face like just another face. Then he saw in those almond-shaped eyes the sorrow he had sought words for. He knew he loved her. More than ever. He nodded. "Yeah. I want to know."

"He won't tolerate your presence around here when I tell him. The father of my unborn child."

Again, he nodded. Then words came to him. "I think I know how he would've felt."

"Do you? And do you know how I feel?"

He crimped his lips. "I wish I knew."

"I must live with the guilt that I've put you through all this."

"Is that all?"

She pursed her lips like she was stuck with thoughts. Then she let out a deep sigh.

"You have no feeling for me?" he said.

"What do you think?" Her voice was nearly inaudible. "Must I speak it?"

"That's what I thought," he said, hearing the muted pain in her voice.

She looked down at the linoleum floor, sighed, and looked back up at him. "You must leave tomorrow morning. Your foreman will drive you into town. Once I tell my husband tonight, he will want you out of here."

"I can leave any time. I'm more worried about you."

"I can take care of myself. May I ask where you'll be headed?"

"I don't know." He smiled. "I wish I knew."

"Is that the truth?"

"I never lie. At least that's what we have in common."

"Only that much?" Her eyes were half closed with the familiar softness he knew well.

He drew a deep breath. "Sometimes," he said, "what isn't said says a lot more."

After she left, he took a bath and then went to the barn to saddle the quarter horse. Her stallion wasn't in its stall. He led the horse out of the stable and down the gravel walk to the gate. As he opened the gate, standing in the cold silver illumination the lamps cast about him, he looked up toward the second-floor veranda where the railing etched quietly in white against the night. The wheelchair wasn't there.

Night dew had wet the sand, and the water in the pond by the parsnip field looked pale in the moonlight. Toads croaked, their throaty calls echoing in the swale. He stood the horse and gazed at the field. Gone were the breathtaking yellow flowers that dotted the field like a myriad butterflies fluttering. Now their stalks, slender and broken, had browned, and the stubbled field looked sterile. The horse lowered its head to nip at the stalks. Paper-like seeds lay scattered on the ground, and in the stalks fireflies blinked and the field seemed to be speaking to any soul that understood its soundless voice.

He rode along the dirt path toward the lighthouse and up the slope, cresting it under the peaceful creamy moonlight that bathed the sea, the dunes. In the breeze the whistling pines smelled of dried cones now lying like well-worn rocks among a mat of rusty red needles. When they shed and paved the ground thickly, the children of the hamlets would come and rake them and bag them for firewood. The air then filled with a pleasant odor.

He rode down the slope through a patch of goat's foot vine, the horse snorting heavily, kicking up sand as they crossed a long tract carpeted with evening primrose flowering pink and white. Among them, dune sunflowers rose tall and yellow as the moon. The sea breeze brought in their heady scent, so thick he had to breathe through his mouth to clear his head.

Wolf spiders were coming out of their burrows in the sand where the horse stood grazing. He watched them push out the tiny pebbles they plugged their holes with against floodwater. He turned the horse back, heeled it hard, and it took off like something crazed. He was riding hard until farther up the shore he saw her white horse standing on the watermark the waves left, and up on the sand she was sitting, her knees drawn up to her chin, her hands hugging her knees.

When he reined up he couldn't hear his own breathing for the heavy snorting of his horse. He got down.

"Hi," he said as he took off his sandals and stood holding them in his hands.

"Hi," she said, lowering her head to rest her chin on her knees. She was barefoot in her tight blue jeans. The breeze fluttered the loose sleeves of her white shirt.

"I thought you'd never come out this way again," he said, standing in one place as his horse found its friend and now stood side by side with the stallion.

"I thought the same about you."

"Well, looks like we have to say goodbye one more time."

"One more time, yes." She didn't brush back the stray hair the breeze left tangled on her face.

"I wished that you'd be out here. But, well, I also wished that you wouldn't."

That drew a faint smile from her. "Why?"

"I don't know why. Maybe it'd be very hard to say goodbye again."

"I imagine so." Then she gazed up at him. "Why don't you sit down with me?"

He placed his sand-coated sandals between his feet, sitting with his arms cradling his knees next to her. The breeze brought an herbal fragrance from her hair, and suddenly he felt lightheaded.

"How's the boy doing?" he asked without looking at her.

"He's fine," she said. "I don't know what to tell him when he notices that you're gone."

"How could you tell that he could tell?"

"I just know."

"You want me to give him the myna?"

"No. If there's someone you want to give it to, it's me." She smiled a gentle smile.

"Then it's yours. It can say your name very clearly. It said, 'Where's Ly now' after you left tonight."

"No, keep it. I don't want it to remind me of something that'd haunt me."

He gazed out toward the distant mud flats, dark and shimmering. The blind man wasn't in sight.

The first time he knew about the blind man, he was riding on the beach with her, and she raised her arm and pointed toward a small figure, slumped and pale in the moonlight, working on a sand flat halfway between them and a bonfire. The figure moved a hand net along the wet sand, a basket hoisted on the hip. "See that person?" she said. "He's blind."

"I see him."

"He's from the hamlet. Born blind. He picks clams

and fish, those dropped by fishing nets when they haul them out of the boats in the late afternoon."

"I guess he never needs a light on the beach to do what he does."

"No. Just needs to be aware of the tide cycle and the moon cycle. You don't want to be swept away by high tide when you're out here by yourself at night. He told me every night he goes out and away from the hamlet as far as he can, until his ears no longer pick up any sound from the hamlet. He did get lost sometimes though. Told me when that happened he had to rely on his nose to smell the wind, even use his tongue to test the wind to find his way back."

Now she caught him gazing and said, "What's out there?"

"I guess I wouldn't see him again before I leave tonight."

"Who?"

"The blind man."

"It'll be late when he's out there during high tide."

"Sometimes I caught fish out that way and just threw them back in the water because he wasn't there." Then he shook his head. "His is a different world."

She broke her gaze with a nod of her head. "Ours too."

"You and me?"

"Your world and mine."

"You know what I often wish for?"

"You're a man of few words so I'd be delighted to hear."

"That when I met you, you were just an ordinary girl from a poor home like me."

"What made you think that would work out for you

and me?"

"You'd have nothing to give up."

"You've never said you love me."

He looked into her eyes, gentle and demure, and in that moment, he saw the graceful softness that had melted his heart once all over again. "I love you," he said. "But it's never easy for me to say it."

She leaned her forehead against his and, her eyes closed, touched his face with her hand. "Do you regret that you met me?"

"No." He tried to smile. "I learned from you to like surprises."

"Did you really?"

"Do you regret it?"

She shook her head and put her finger on his lips. Her face felt cold against his, and the fragrance of her hair brought him the very name of sorrow.

* * *

He woke twice when the boat docked to let off passengers and pick up new ones. Night riders who came on board as quietly as thieves, their clothes rustling, some carrying nothing while others lugging with them all kinds of merchandise. Once, past midnight, the boat docked and ferry peddlers sang out their food choices from the landing. The woman woke, looking around in the faint reflection of lights from the food stalls.

"Where are we?" she asked him.

"I don't know." He craned his neck looking out toward the pier. "Aren't you hungry?"

"No. I brought food with me. Would you like some?"

"No, thanks. If I eat now, I'll stay awake for a while."

"You mean you want to save your stomach for what she has for you at home."

"Well …"

"Does she know you'll be home soon?"

"Yeah."

"Aren't you excited?"

"I am. I mean, knowing she's home waiting."

"You forgot the little one inside her, too."

"Oh yeah."

"You can't go anywhere long enough without thinking of them."

"You tell me. You've been there before."

"Yes. I've been there before." She lay her cheek on her daughter's head and smiled. After a while she said, "Where are you exactly on the Plain?"

"Where?" He cocked his head to one side. "You know where the canal ends into the Plain?"

"Hmm. I think I know where."

"I'm somewhere around there."

"Maybe someday I'll take my daughter there to visit you. She loves horses."

"Sure." He looked back out to the landing and the woman, at his silence, didn't inquire further of his whereabouts. Then he said to her, "When will we arrive?"

"By early morning. I thought you knew that."

"Well, not exactly. This is my first time away from home."

"You can't wait to get home to see her again, can you?"

"Yeah."

"I'm happy for you."

"Thanks."

Soon the riverboat was moving again. He slept, and

when he woke, he could see the velvety black of the night glowing with myriad tiny lights, yellow and green: fireflies in the trees, lining the banks. He watched those stars until the boat left them behind. In his sleep he smelled the strong earthy scent of horses and heard the sound of waves and, waking again, saw that a gray tint in the sky, and the banks yellow with river hemp in bloom. Among them were the gnarled trunks, like black giants, of mangrove trees. It was drizzling and the wind came up from the land. He could smell the cajeput flowers and soon he saw them, tiny and white, crowding the riverbank, their trunks wetly black like buffalo horns. The Plain now came into view, flat, immense, and steely gray, boundless, brimming with floodwater. Past clumps of bushwillows with their tops above the water, he heard moorhens calling, and rain falling and popping like packets of broken needles on the surface of the water, the wind damp. In that grayness, a heron rose into the air.

The riverboat found the ferry landing in the rain. The woman woke up her daughter.

"We're here, sweetie," she said to the girl.

The girl rubbed her eyes and looked toward the landing. "Is daddy there waiting for us?"

"He'll be there." She picked up the birdcage from her daughter's lap and gave it to him. "Well, we're getting off here. Yours is the next stop, I guess."

"You're right."

The girl pulled the cloth just to peek at the myna. "Hello baby," she said.

"Hello," the myna said.

"He never sleeps, does he?" she asked him.

"He does."

"I'll miss him, I know I will."

As they stood up, he said to them, "Wait."

They looked down at him. He took the girl's hands and put the birdcage in them. "Kim," he said, "you take him home with you now, okay? Take care of him."

"Oh my," she said.

The woman smiled, shaking her head. "You're spoiling her now."

"Teach him something new every day," he said to the girl.

"Will he forget what you've taught him?"

"He won't. He's a very smart bird."

"Would he say, 'Thank you, Ly' when I feed him?"

"You tell him your name. That's all you do, hear?"

"Will he love me like he loves her?"

"I'm sure he will. He needs affection. Like us."

"Thank you so much!"

He sat back, hands on his thighs. "You all have a good day now."

"You'll be home soon yourself," the woman said, tapping him on the shoulder.

"Yeah," he said, smiling at her, "home."

After they departed from the boat, he leaned his head against the sash and gazed across the water. Farther up he could see a huge mangrove tree, gnarled and shaggy, rising out of the water like an ancient landmark. Beyond it, a house, a small dark shape on the low, gray horizon. And beyond that, the final destination of an unnamed landing where the riverboat would stop.

He heard the little girl calling out to her father on the landing and then the myna's croaking voice, "Hello guest."

The rain was coming down hard. It was the rainy season again.

Two Shores

I came to know Dr. Đàm from our reeducation camp after he received a diatribe from a lecturer one morning. As a bona fide medical doctor in the Republic of Vietnam Army, Dr. Đàm now served these northern nurses, appointed as medical doctors by the Communist Party, and watched them treat the sick, the near-death patients. He must have felt as if he was living in the nineteenth century.

Holding up a book, the political lecturer said, "All the historical truths about the Democratic Republic of Vietnam and its allies are written in this textbook." He showed us the cover. *History of the August Revolution.* "All the truths fabricated by the American imperialists and your puppet government are corrected in this primer. For example, the Imperial Army of Japan surrendered to our ally, the Soviet Union, in Manchuria, which ended Japan's expansionist dreams."

Dr. Đàm raised his hand. Allowed to speak, he said, "Sir cadre, Japan surrendered to the Allies after the United States dropped two atomic bombs on them, one on Hiroshima and the other Nagasaki. It is not a fabricated fact but a world fact, because every country in the world has this fact in its history textbook."

The cadre's hand holding the book slashed the air up and down. "There you go again. Of course, those nations are in cahoots with the American imperialists.

But you are a discontented element, one who spoke ill of our Revolution with your anti-propaganda and reactionary misinformation." He pointed at Dr. Đàm. "What was your former profession with the puppet government?"

"Sir cadre," Dr. Đàm said softly, "I was conscripted into the army during the First Republic and served through the Second Republic as a military physician. I was a major."

"A major," said the lecturer, snorting. "For over a decade you treated the sick and the wounded soldiers of the rebel government. You committed the unforgivable crime of strengthening the puppet regime. But you are not going to be brought to trial. That's the saving grace. Otherwise, you would be tried under our original laws enacted by the Democratic Republic of Vietnam, under which you would be imprisoned from three to twelve years for propagandizing the enslavement policy and depraved culture of imperialism."

I found out later that Dr. Đàm was a member of the vegetable team. Yet Dr. Đàm was frail and plagued with eye trouble. One morning I had diarrhea and, as I went to the infirmary, I passed through the alley between the two dwellings of the camp personnel. I saw him raking the ground. I stopped and asked him, "What are you doing here, sir?"

"I'm preparing the ground to grow sweet potato vine for our cadres," he said.

I rubbed my abdomen. "By the way, do you think our infirmary have antibiotics?" I had seen him work there occasionally whenever the nurses desperately needed a professional opinion on certain treatments.

"Your guess is as good as mine. Are you ailing?"

I told him.

He said nothing, quietly returning to his chores by continuing to rake the ground softly.

I arrived at the infirmary. There was already a line of five men outside. The familiar young male nurse was on call, sitting behind a wooden table which kept wobbling every time he leaned on it. He looked hostile, as if those standing in line were about to rob him. My turn came.

"May I have medication for diarrhea?" I asked.

"I have none. Next."

I went back to my shack, passing through the alley, and ran into Dr. Đàm again. He leaned on his rake, squinting at me. "Any luck?"

I shook my head. He appraised me with his rheumy eyes. "I'll ask around. Somebody might have antibiotics. By the way, what exactly did you ask him?"

"I said, 'May I have medication for diarrhea?'"

"That's why you got none. You played the doctor's role. You should let him be the doctor, and you the patient. Ask, 'Sir Doctor, I don't know why my stomach keeps twisting in pain and I let it out several times a day. Just watery discharge each time.' He'd say, 'That's diarrhea.' Understand? Play dumb. Let them be smart."

In time, I grew fond of him. A medical doctor with compassion. When the camp had allowed inmates to write home, most of us asked our families to buy the things we needed most to treat our illnesses. I was in the security shack where letters and parcels were opened and inspected. Dr. Đàm received a gift from home. One of the security cadres, holding up the small glass vial, asked him, "What is this liquid?" It was amber brown.

"For my gastric ulcer, sir cadre," he said.

"What is gastric ulcer?" the cadre asked.

"Have you ever had constant stomach pains?"

The cadre looked quizzical at Dr. Đàm and shook his head.

"Such pains are often caused by gastric ulcers," Dr. Đàm said. "They come about when stomach acid causes open sores on the lining of the stomach."

Still looking quizzical, the cadre opened the vial, sniffed, then flicked his eyes at Dr. Đàm. "What is it made of?"

Dr. Đàm pointed at the vial in the cadre's hand but avoided his stare. "It's made mainly of honey and herbal extracts. Southern folk medicine, sir cadre."

"You people from the South have all kinds of unorthodox things, as far as I know." The cadre reluctantly gave the vial back to Dr. Đàm.

If Dr. Đàm had told him, as he had later told us once we were outside the security shack, that it was bear bile, which he needed to treat inmates for internal injuries caused by beatings, then he would have been sent to a penal cell and had his family gift confiscated.

The few times I stayed in the sick bay, I saw him work with the camp's antiquated medical equipment during surgery. Nobody from the camp personnel knew how to operate those devices: the autoclave that was used to sterilize equipment, the Ombredanne Inhaler for administering anesthesia. They dated to World War I. With these devices, he once performed an appendicostomy on a patient, attaching his colon to his belly button in order to give him the enema for severe constipation. When so many inmates suffered edema, and the camp's infirmary had no cure for it, Dr. Đàm simply asked the cadre in charge of the kitchen to spare him every day a share of pig's mash. He made our edema victims eat it to give their body a dose of much-needed vitamin B1.

Because of his poor eyesight, Dr. Đàm would diagnose a patient by taking his pulse and asking him to describe his symptoms. Three typical cases among the inmates established his reputation and caught the camp's attention. One patient was a noted South Vietnam novelist, whose ailment was stomach cancer; another was a former senior officer of South Vietnam Ministry of Chiêu Hồi – Open Arms – who had hepatitis; and another was a former director of the South Vietnam Central Intelligence Office, who had diabetes. The first two eventually died from cancer and hepatitis; the third still lived, perhaps never forgetting Dr. Đàm's humorous remark: "The worst offender to diabetes is glucose. It comes from sugar. White rice causes spikes in blood sugar, which is bad for diabetes. But rest assured, you won't have to be on any diet for your ailment. How often do we get white rice here? How frequently do we receive sugar as a treat?"

The camp officials knew he was an authentic M.D., for he was a former military doctor with a major rank. But they never called him "doctor." Smiling, he once said to me, "They regard me as a nurse. Just out of an inferiority complex." Then he added, "These medical doctors they brought in from the North were abysmally ignorant. Let's start with their education system. It's ten years from elementary to high school, not twelve like in our academic system. Those who studied medicine spent two, three years in medical school and then were rushed to the battlefield. Their reference sources came from Russian books, none from western sources, much less American or British or French. Even with the aid of French medical books, many of them couldn't read French." He looked around then back at me, softening his voice. "You know why we don't have more medical doctors in any of these camps who came from our former administration? They were released and brought to Saigon to help those idiotic commies run the hospitals. The commies didn't trust their own doctors."

In the camp's infirmary, where he was called in occasionally to help, there was one cot reserved for him to display his medical instruments, all of them manufactured by us, the inmates, from scrap metal we scavenged from the GMC trucks the North had transported home after the war. Those scavenging days were miserable. Imagine carrying back all kinds of scrap metal in your sacks, so heavy your knees nearly buckled, as you trod in the spine-tingling heat at high noon. Out of those scraps, our smithy produced some heavy-duty pliers. Dr. Đàm used them, one day, to pull out one of my molars. Fortunately for me, one of my fellow inmates had donated a tube of local anesthetic but, even with the numbing effect, the reduction of pain was minimal, and I passed out.

One day, I saw Dr. Đàm working among us in the manioc field, because the camp had pulled many inmates from other teams to speed up the harvest. I stopped pulling up the tubers and went to him. "Why are you here, sir?" I asked him.

"Lost my status," he said, then continued. "Remember the visit last week from the Central Committee? Those inspectors they sent to our camp? I was flanked by our camp security when those men came to inquire about the camp living conditions. I'd been briefed to lie like a commie. Before I knew it, I said to those inspectors, 'All we have here to combat malaria is a limited quantity of quinine, and it came from the inmates who got them

from our former administration. What we have in camp from the Revolution is herbal medicine, and the one we use mostly is that *Xuyên Tâm Liên*, the King of Bitters, as our panacea. That cure-all medicine does nothing to stop illnesses. As far as hygiene goes, our infirmary sits by our camp fertilizer shack where we store human waste from the latrines to feed our vegetables. The permanent odor in the infirmary is unhealthy to our patients. Moreover, the human waste as fertilizer leaves bacteria on our vegetables and causes sickness if not washed thoroughly.'"
He shook his head as I understood the consequence of his outburst.

Moments after I went back to pulling manioc tubers from the ground, I heard his voice coming over. He was singing:

Arise, the damned of the world!
Arise, all the hungry people!

I stood up and saw the overseer walking toward him. "Why did you sing that song?" he asked our doctor.

"Sir cadre," said Dr. Đàm, "I was singing *The International*, the first Soviet Union national anthem. It's an official Socialist and Communist song."

"But why did you sing just the first two lines? Who rise up? Who? While you're laboring as such?"

"I memorized only those two lines. Whenever I'm tired, I sing those two lines. It's effective, sir cadre. It restores my enthusiasm for the Revolution."

"Liar! That song is holy to our Socialist State, to the world proletariat. You can't sing it with just two lines. It proves that you're lacking the spirit of reforming yourself."

The next morning, I did not see him during our roll call in the dirt courtyard. By evening, I learned that he was being detained in a penal cell, with both feet shack-led.

* * *

What saved Dr. Đàm from the calamity of the penal cell, considering his age, was a word from the camp's security chief who sent for him. I did not see Dr. Đàm for three days. I was worried. I asked Mr. Thạch, a close friend of Dr. Đàm, and his equanimity put me at ease. "Brother Khang, what would become of this world without med-ical doctors?"

The next day, to my surprise, Dr. Đàm joined our manioc harvesting team. Both he and Mr. Thạch were out on the field shoveling dirt, pulling up roots, and cut-ting off tubers. I looked over at the two old men and sup-pressed my outburst of enmity toward the wardens. That day, we had packed our meals when we left camp at day-break. We were to stay at the work site without returning to camp for lunch. The three of us – me, Mr. Thạch, and Dr. Đàm – sat under the shade of a hornbeam. Before I brought out my Guigoz can which contained my lunch – half *bo bo* and half yellow corn – Dr. Đàm said, "Save them. Let's enjoy our socialist premium porridge."

He set two *goz* cans on the grass. He opened one can and I the other. Inside was white porridge, thick and creamy. Dr. Đàm retrieved three tin cups from his sack as I watched him, wide-eyed. "Where are all these from, sir?" I asked.

"The cups?" He flicked a smile. "From the kitchen, courtesy of our camp's security chief." He poured the content of one *goz* can into the cups. "This porridge is no ordinary porridge. Taste it."

We spooned porridge into our mouths. I paused. It tasted sweet. A fine sweetness, not as coarse as with granular sugar. Dr. Đàm nodded. "That's cane sugar. The finest. Only for the camp's higher-ups."

Mr. Thạch snickered. "Like the security chief?"

"Yes," Dr. Đàm grinned, blinking.

"What's the story here, sir?" I asked.

"The chief sent for me," Dr. Đàm said. He paused to taste the porridge and smacked his lips. "This is just right, not too sweet. Agreeable to everyone?"

We nodded. Dr. Đàm continued. "I assumed the worst when their doctor – the head nurse from the infirmary – came to fetch me. We went to the chief's dwelling. By the door there was a wire cage framed by sturdy-looking bamboo trunks. Inside, there was a black python coiled up on its white-striped, yellow belly. The head nurse said it was the chief's pet. He said guards would catch rats to feed this reptile. I smelled a stink."

Dr. Đàm poured more porridge into Mr. Thạch's cup, which was near empty. Mine was still half full. "Have you ever seen the chief?" Dr. Đàm asked. "No? Neither have I. I heard he rarely showed his face during the day. Most of his work, including inspecting the security of the camp, was carried out at night. A fearsome figure even to his own people."

Dr. Đàm put down his cup and rubbed his eyes. Overhead, a finch tweeted. It must have come to feed on the hornbeam's nutlets. Dr. Đàm continued. "I've heard from guards that he was the one that bashed the heads of our escapees, and ordered their corpses to be displayed on the courtyard for us to behold. I wasn't too eager to meet him. After the head nurse announced my arrival at the door, I heard a voice: 'Enter.' A heavy northern accent.

I'm a southerner, and if there's an accent that puts me on guard it's a northern accent – not just any northern accent like yours, Brother Khang, and my friend Thạch's – but one that's heavy like from a backwater. We entered.

"It was the first time I saw his face. Shocked, I was. The interior was dim, but the face I saw was disfigured, its left side all shiny scars. His left ear was missing. He gestured for me to sit and dismissed the head nurse. That damaged left side affected him when he spoke, like someone was pinching the corner of his mouth. That's when I noticed his left hand. It had four fingers missing, and his left arm was all scarred. I wouldn't guess what had happened to him until later. But let me get to the point."

By then I had finished my cup at the same as Mr. Thạch did. We received more porridge. Dr. Đàm still had his cup part full. He continued.

"The chief said to me, 'My daughter has come to visit me from Hanoi. She has complained about stomach pains on and off, even though in Hanoi she received treatments from one of our medical doctors. But the pains came back. I want you to diagnose her symptoms and come up with a remedy.' The chief called into an interior room, and his daughter came out. She must have been eighteen or nineteen. Sweet, innocent looking girl. A little pale though.

"The chief made a fist and brought it down onto the table, like when you rubber-stamp a document. He said, 'If you cause harm to her, I will see to it that you pay for your ineptitude.' I said to him, 'Sir cadre, I'm a physician. I cure people, not harm them.' The chief stood up, giving up his chair for his daughter. I said to her, 'When you have a bowel movement, what is the color of your stool?' She looked perplexed. Embarrassed, maybe.

I repeated my question. She said, 'It was dark.' 'Recently, or was it like that in Hanoi?' I asked. 'Very recently,' she said.

"I asked for a pen and a piece of paper and said to the chief, 'She has stomach ulcers. Her dark stool is due to bleeding. If left untreated it'll cause holes through the wall of the stomach.' I glanced at her. She looked alarmed. The chief said, 'If you can treat her, you will deserve my praise. It is not a small matter, though it was malpractice on that doctor's part.' 'Yes, sir cadre. I'm going to write you a prescription. The two drugs: one will reduce acid to help heal the ulcer; the other is liquid medication to help cover the ulcer with a protective layer to prevent further damage from the acids.'

"The chief appeared relaxed and said, 'What about her daily nutrition? Anything that will help in her daily meals?' 'Yes, sir cadre. Put her on a brown-rice porridge diet and drink brown-rice extract after it's roasted – do not overly roast it. There are vitamins, fiber, minerals, and protein in brown rice bran to help cope with stomach ulcer.'"

Overhead, the finch tweeted again then flew off. Dr. Đàm ate two spoonfuls and continued.

"He asked me to stay at the infirmary until he summoned me. After three days, he sent for me again – that was yesterday. He said, 'My daughter is free of pain now. She can eat without feeling discomfort, but she remains on a brown rice diet. The medicine worked wonders for her.' I said to him, 'Have her on that diet and continue taking medication for the next seven days. These ten days are critical. Do not miss medication and do not eat anything else but brown rice, and drink brown rice extract.' He gave me a small carton. Inside there was granulated cane sugar. I could tell it was of good quality. He said, 'Tell the kitchen to spare you one kilo of white rice. Ask them to cook it for you, or you can cook at your leisure without being questioned by your shack leader or trusty or warden. You are a good doctor.'"

Such largesse, I thought.

A finch came to perch on a branch above my head. I could not tell if it was the one from before or a different finch.

Mr. Thạch lit a cigarette. "That chief is something to be reckoned with, isn't he?" He squinted behind the coils of smoke. "What happened to his face anyway?"

Dr. Đàm set his cup down on the grass. "From what his daughter told me – under her breath when he was out of sight – it came from the war. Artillery fragments during a battle in Pleiku." He licked the spoon clean, shaking his head. "That's my hometown. Fortunately, he must've not read my self-confession. The daughter said her father used to be handsome in his youth. Well, I couldn't be the judge of that. I never wanted to look at him squarely. He seemed to prefer darkness, and there's certainly something ominous about him. She asked me if I could think of any medication to help restore some of his facial qualities. I said I wasn't God. I wasn't sure if she was brought up as an atheist, fearing no God, respecting no one except those goons from the Party. I told her if her mother accepted him for who he was, that was that."

Mr. Thạch nodded but said nothing. I chimed in. "Did you see his wife?"

Dr. Đàm slowly capped one of the empty *goz* cans and peered up at me. "She was killed during the American bombing in 1972. They bombed Hanoi, Hải Phòng, Lạng Sơn, Bắc Giang, and Thái Nguyên. His family is from Thái Nguyên. I didn't say anything when she told me that; but I thought if their family had lived within ten miles from the border of China, her mother would've lived."

That was the buffer zone, I thought, as Dr. Đàm went on. "She was twelve years old then when her mother died, and she lived with her maternal grandparents while he was fighting in the South. I could tell he hated us, the people he'd fought against."

I thought of our two escape comrades who had died from gruesome head wounds, whose bodies were buried without coffins. It was barely a month since three prisoners had escaped. They had a gun with them. Nobody knew how they had secured it. But one guard had been killed by a gunshot when the escapees fired back during the chase.

That same afternoon the gong called us back earlier than usual. At four o'clock, the sun still bright before the descending fog, we arrived at the camp just in time to see the guards bring out the bodies of the captives. One look at them knotted my stomach. They were still tied by their hands and feet like pigs being carried to the market. Their heads were misshapen: the temples dented, the hair matted down with dark blood, the eyes not even seated in their own sockets. One man's jaw was askew. I found it hard to breathe and felt the same horror in everyone else around me. The dead had been violated by direct blows to the heads by some blunt instrument; blood still oozed from the head wounds. The guards had not even bothered to reseat the eyeballs. The dead man with the displaced jaw had his face turned toward where I sat on the ground. His face was a horror mask of welts and bruises with dangling eyeballs.

To make sure we had time to contemplate the scene, with its graphic display, the administrator waited. Then he spoke.

"On behalf of our security committee and the proctor committee, I ask for a brief moment of silence to pay respects to our deceased guard, who put his life at risk when he went after the offenders." He dropped his head, closing his eyes while afternoon sunlight gilded his face. We followed his gesture. I put my mind on our dead comrades, not knowing what to say or pray. Words meant nothing. The administrator lifted his face and squinted at us. "We now close the book on this regrettable incident. The camp suffers one casualty. But our security forces never fail in their duties. They shot and killed one of the offenders in the forest, the one who had wielded a gun. Now know this: once you kill our personnel, there is no going back. Look at this incident, remember it, memorize this scene today, then ask yourself: What can I do under the guidance of the Party and the State to shed my old self, and become a model citizen?" He pointed at the corpses. "On behalf of Cổng Trời camp and the intercamp authority, I hereby issue the edict of having these criminals buried without coffins."

I felt fortunate that it was a senior lieutenant who had interrogated and later worked with me on my self-confession. Had it been this man, the security chief, I could have received a different treatment. Then I thought it could be his disfigured appearance that had deterred him from showing himself in public. My stream of thought broke when Dr. Đàm tapped me on the shoulder again.

"Brother Khang, you'll have to go with me now to the chief's quarter. You're needed there."

Alarmed, I looked quizzically at him. "Why me?"

Dr. Đàm smiled. "Easy now. It's the daughter. She liked this Russian song and wanted to read its lyrics in English. She said she loved the English language, and I thought of you."

"You told the chief I could transcribe the words?"

"Literally, yes." Dr. Đàm chuckled. "Not transliterating, of course."

"I don't know Russian from Chinese. How could I translate for her?"

"Don't worry. She's translated the lyrics from Russian to Vietnamese. Now all you'll have to do is go from Vietnamese to English."

Mr. Thạch snickered. "If you can't, he'll feed you to his python."

* * *

Dr. Đàm and I entered the chief's house. I could smell a bad odor from the python as I crossed the threshold. The interior was dim. The chief sat in a chair farther into the unlit corner as he listened to his daughter playing her violin. The music was melodious, a tune I could not recognize.

Dr. Đàm introduced me to the chief, who remained in the shadow, and to his daughter, who rose politely and bowed to us, a gesture I had never seen among the northerners who had discriminated against us after the war. It helped soften my feeling toward her, and I bowed back. I could not make out the chief's face, nor did I want to look at him. The girl took me to a small round table near the door where sunlight fell on its brown wood on which lay scattered sheets of music and white sheets of paper. She picked up a sheet with writing scribbled on it.

"This song," she said in her melodious northern accent, "was written by a Russian songwriter named Andrei Yakovlevich Eshpai. I know the Russian language, but I would love to see the lyrics in English. I plan to study English when I return to Hanoi."

I read her handwriting of the song's translation in Vietnamese. 'Two Shores' was the title. I read it from beginning to end and looked at her. She did not have the paleness Dr. Đàm had mentioned. Perhaps the pre-scribed medication had helped restore some of her vitality. She looked fresh.

"May I ask," I said to her, "if you can play this song again just to give me some sense, some feeling for it?"

"Much obliged," she said as she returned to her chair and picked up her violin.

I stood by Dr. Đàm, listening to the undulating notes of the tune. All the time, I avoided looking toward the shadowed corner. Yet I could feel his gaze on us. He must have compared me to those escapees whose lives he took. My gut trembled. Perhaps I was still alive because I did not kill any guards in my only failed escape. I still did not know his name, but it was better that way and I'd rather remain a persona non grata after I had paid the price. But the music. It sounded like our Yellow Music of the South, which the Communists had banned throughout the country after winning. They, the North, reveled in Red Music which exalted its political-military power. I heard that, to the northern victors, Yellow Music, the slow-tempo music in bolero, ballad, and rumba sung in the South, represented decadence, melancholy. This tune I was listening to was mellow. Something sentimental in it stirred a yearning in me. Perhaps something unretriev-able of my long gone past. I read the lyrics again and, half bent with a pen in hand, began turning them into English, guided by the mood I was in.

Rain, rain, all night
On the dewy grass.
People said I'm in love
And I believe them
Though, not true, says my heart.
You and I are two shores
Between us a river.
Rain, rain, all night
Dawn is coming.
I am waiting
Though, no, says my heart.
You and I are two shores
Between us a river.

She asked me to read it aloud. I read it out loud and in one moment felt as if I was speaking about my fate. Me and my family, the two shores. She seemed taken by the words spoken to her, saying she loved the sound of the English language. Momentarily, I forgot the shadowed man in the corner. When I finished, he rose, and his daughter bowed to me and Dr. Đàm again. I bowed back, saying from the bottom of my heart that I loved the song rendered by her performance. In that moment, I felt no division, no barrier between us, of the North and the South, of the captor and the captive.

When we left, she stood in the doorway waving goodbye. The smell of the python followed me. Her father remained inside, in that somber interior. If I were him, living forever defaced, how could I bear it?